THE RUNNING SOUL

MY JOURNEY FROM DARKNESS TO LIGHT

EMBASSY BOOKS
www.embassybooks.in

PARUL SHETH

The Running Soul

Copyright © 2015 Parul Sheth

This edition first published in 2015

First Published in India by :

EMBASSY BOOK DISTRIBUTORS
120, Great Western Building,
Maharashtra Chamber of Commerce Lane,
Fort, Mumbai - 400 023.
Tel : (+91-22) 22819546 / 32967415
Email : info@embassybooks.in
Website: www.embassybooks.in

ISBN : 978-93-83359-69-1

ABOUT THE AUTHOR

Parul Sheth is a fulltime mother, fulltime runner, fulltime architect and a novice writer. This book is the story of how she began as a non-runner, who trained, evolved as a person and a marathoner and ran the race of her life at the age of 42 in the 2014 Standard Chartered Mumbai Marathon. Over the last 10 years, she has brought up 2 teenagers as a single parent, worked as an architect designing restaurants, and developed herself as an individual with several hobbies and a whole new life.

She has run 3 marathons, 14 half marathons and several other races

ACKNOWLEDGEMENTS

My life has been shaped by so many people. A lot of you have been included in this book, but by no means, all. I am indebted to each and every one of you for your unconditional support, friendship, love, inspiration and guidance.

First and foremost, I would like to thank my family for their unflinching support in all my crazy ventures. My in-laws, my parents, my sister Rima. Thanks to my sisters and brothers-in-law, aunts, uncles and cousins for providing the family cocoon of love. They have always come out in full force for all my runs, at odd hours to cheer me on, and have been there for me through thick and thin. They have looked after my children when I have been out running. I have been able to become a runner thanks to them.

A BIG thank you to my running family. Each of you could have easily been a dedicated chapter! And the ones that I have not named, it is out of worry of this book becoming too long! There is much that I have learnt from all of you. Thank you Savio's Stars.

Each and every one of you.

Thank you, Ashwitha, my editor, for polishing the book and making it into a complete story. A big thank you to Anita, without whose support I would have been lost in the publishing world. A special mention for Sukhpreet, Amee, Nikita and Maithili for having knocked sense into my head when I needed it and for keeping me grounded. Thanks to Meera for a book design which reflected my personality, Amee for the inspired cover and to Ashima, for the flattering photographs.

I wish Udayan Patel was here to see this book come to life. He would have been proud of me. He will always have my heartfelt gratitude.

To Mr. Cooper and Sandeep for continually inspiring me to do my best.

It is my privilege to have Nanditaben as a friend to smile with and as a mentor who showed me the way, who encouraged me when I lost faith in myself.

I will always be grateful to Savio D'Souza for my evolution from a runner into a marathoner. This transition would not have been possible without you.

PREFACE *by Amit Sheth*

I first met Parul at a party which was being hosted by a fellow runner. I remember a cheerful young woman, full of life, listening to me with rapt attention as I expounded my theories on Marathon running. At the end of my long dissertation, she asked me what my plans were for the Mumbai Marathon, which was just a few weeks away. I explained to her that I was pacing the sub 5 bus.

She asked me about my strategy for race day. I explained to her that the 42.2km of the marathon road is much like "Life's Battlefield". I told her that I would start right at the back-end of the race and help the runners reach the finish just under 5:00 hours.
She said that she would think about joining me, as she had a similar time goal. But although she said that she would join me, my instinct told me otherwise.

As we left the party, Neepa, my wife, told me that I should have kept my mouth shut and not said anything about "Life's Battlefields" to Parul. She told me that Parul had been through enough tragedy in her personal life that my little 42.2km battlefield analogy would hold no dread for her.

After listening to Parul's story from Neepa, I was sure that I would not see Parul on race day. I had realised that this was a woman who charges into life's battles, leading from the front. She would not start with me at the back end of the race. She is a warrior who is willing to take on life by the horns. It does not matter what the challenge is.

So, I never did meet Parul on race day. She started at the front end of her seeding and finished the race far ahead of me. I was so proud of her.

Like me, Parul is a recreational runner. And as a recreational runner, I have a slightly different yardstick to judge a fellow runner. For me, any person who loves to run, is a runner. A good runner, is one who not only loves to run but also is regular in training. A great runner, for me, is one who is not only a good runner but also someone who is willing to motivate and help other runners. By this yardstick, Parul is an exceptionally great runner.

Very often, on a Sunday Morning, as I trained for the Comrades ultra marathon 2014, I would meet Parul on the road. I would be about 80% done with my long run and would consequently be quite tired. Without batting an eyelid, she would turn and join me, so as to pace me, for the remaining length of my run. The fact that this disrupted her own run did not seem to bother her. To me, that is the sign of a great runner.

The pages which follow tell the story of her runs in the Mumbai and other Marathons around India. They also tell the story of an exceptional woman who has overcome daunting odds in her personal life. It is a story which awes and inspires. If you are not a runner, this story makes you want to run. If you are a runner, this story makes you want to dare to do more.

I do not know what challenges and battlefields Parul will have to face in the future. But one thing i know for certain. Whenever life's battlefield calls, this is a woman who will lead into battle.

Amit B Sheth
Author: ***Dare to Run***

DEDICATION

For my children, Arnav and Sanjana,
who were the light in my world of darkness;
And for Savio, who showed me the way when I was lost.

The hourglass *indicates a change in time...*
Moving from the current 2014 race to a thought back in time

The road *marks a change in the line of thought*

CONTENTS

Acknowledgements *6*
Preface *8*

THE WARM UP *15*

1: **The Start** *22*
2: **The Story** *35*
3: **Frailty and Strength** *44*
4: **Rebirth** *53*
5: **Endurance** *72*
6: **Goal and Strategy** *84*
7: **Fear and Readiness** *101*

MAP *115*

Epilogue *117*
Tips for new runners *121*

In January 2004, five months after an event that changed my life forever, the first Standard Chartered Mumbai Marathon (SCMM for short) was held.

The 7km or the 21km? That was the question. I had never, ever run before, had not even qualified for a 100m race when I was in school. I had always been fit, though. I had played some sport or the other, or worked out in some form, whether it was aerobics, the magic mantra of the 80s, or jazz dancing with Shiamak in the 90s.

Somehow, come October 2003, I found myself part of a group of three – Ashish, Nimisha R. and I – training for the first ever SCMM half marathon. Ashish and Nimisha R. were old friends and far superior runners, who always ran longer and faster than I could.

I, on the other hand, was usually the one who stopped somewhere along the road to wait for them.

When I started running with them in earnest, I was running from a lot.
Anger.
Pain.
Loss.
Insecurity.

My demons weighed me down. Even the loud music of my iPod couldn't drown them out.

WARM UP

15th January 2014.
Friday: Less than 48 hours to race day.
The hard work is done and only the final remains. "Treat it just like another Sunday run," Savio always says before a race. All those long runs taught us everything that we needed to learn. Over the last 8 months, we had run in the heat, over hills and long distances to build up our endurance. It has taken me a long time to understand what being 'experienced' really means. We tend to take the events in our lives for granted, but each run and each day teaches us something. It is important to assimilate this, because all runs are valuable, especially those in which you find yourself reaching the finish line in a cab instead of on your own two feet. When we need to dig deep in difficult moments, this is the bank of memories from which strength will emerge!
From the tough days and the hard runs, the bad days and the failed runs.

Saturday: 21 hours to race day

I wake up with a catch in my back, which only gets worse during the day. As I obsess over it, it grows, disappears and eventually reappears. I am not prepared for this. I know that I should not try anything new in the hours leading up to race day, but I just have to find a way to deal with the pain. I try to tell myself that I am imagining it. But no, each time I take a deep breath, it hurts. Not a figment of my imagination, then. A sustained release painkiller is the only thing that will do the trick. I spend the afternoon on my back watching "Chariots of Fire" for inspiration. I visualise myself sprinting the last 400m like the 1924 Olympians, with the often played theme song ringing in my ears. Even better are visions of me running in beautiful slow motion across the finish line and coming first! By evening, after a small massage, the pain seems to have subsided.

Sunday: 3.44 am.
The anxiety that the alarm will not ring, wakes me up almost hourly. Adding to the insomnia, are nightmare scenarios about the race floating around in my mind. I should say here that almost all runners are paranoid about their alarms not ringing. This is why we usually have a backup alarm, and a second backup alarm in case the backup alarm fails!

At 3.42 am, I give up trying to sleep. I open my eyes, and lie in bed for another 3 minutes, waiting for the alarm to ring. At 3.44 am, I lose my patience and am up and about. I spend the next half hour preparing: the loo, an oats breakfast, the loo again and a bath (to warm up my muscles). All my running gear is on the desk, having been carefully laid out the previous night. But the craziness continues as I double and triple-check everything.

Once I am dressed, it is time to pin my bib on. There is something about pinning on a number. It is a reminder that you can practice all you like, but what happens on race day is what matters. Running with a bib is bold. It says, yes, I am a runner, and I am putting myself out there in the race for glory.

I am restless now, running around to put the finishing touches to my preparation.
Banana in hand, for last minute energy: check.
Gels (three packets of pre-digested carbohydrate replenishment to be consumed at the stipulated 8, 15 and 25km marks) in my pocket: check.

Water bottle filled to the brim (to hydrate until the start of the race): check.

Hair pinned fiercely away from my face (nothing should distract me!): check.

Vaseline rubbed onto key areas to prevent chaffing (this is critical!): check.

And most importantly, I double-knot those notorious laces to keep them in place! My laces have a habit of coming undone at inconvenient moments: I have strong memories of suffering through the first 800m of my first full marathon in 2011 and the Thane half-marathon in 2009.

The butterflies have begun to flutter.

I review all the details once again before I finally head out of the house, shutting the door behind me.

I am battle ready.

When I return home, I will be a changed person.

Sunday: 4.15am

Vishal picks me up, for the third consecutive year, on the dot at 4.25am. Vishal, Nimisha, Rahul and I, chatter excitedly in the car and within 7 minutes we have reached Metro theatre. We park and walk towards the holding area. On the way, we greet other friends and acquaintants. They are all familiar faces, faces we have seen running alongside us for at least the last 2 months along the Marine Drive and Prabhadevi stretches.

There is motivational banter all around as we walk to Azad Maidan, the historic location of Gandhiji's biggest speech during India's struggle for freedom. Today, it bears witness to individual struggles as we prepare ourselves mentally for the upcoming race. The apprehension is killing me. I am fidgety and cannot wait to reach the starting line, when I will step across the mat and hear the click that will activate my chip, signalling the start of the race. The atmosphere is electric and we are all charged with adrenaline.

Sunday: 5.25 am

The holding area is full of runners of all ages, shapes and sizes: some young guns, a lot of middle-aged ones and a big bunch of seniors. To an observer, this scene would resemble a circus! A gathering of men and women in extremely brightly coloured clothes (plenty of neon!), a lot of people wearing Spandex and looking like trapeze artists! Everyone is in motion, some warming up and stretching. Drinks of all colours are being passed around, hi-fives and cries of "all the best" fill the quiet air of the morning.

This is a happy group, united in their mission, having shared the misery of training, who will strive to complete the whole distance of the marathon to the best of their ability.
One goal. Five thousand people.

It is still dark. Lights flicker around us like fireflies and there is a nip in the air. Heads bob around us as we slow jog towards the start to take our places. These are the last, most unnerving five minutes before the race begins. The glorious and emblematic train station, Chhatrapati Shivaji Terminus, or Victoria Terminus, towers above us in her full glory. A UNESCO world heritage site, the Lady of Progress holds her torch atop the central dome and various celebrities on the podium flag us off.

The loudspeaker is blaring: the countdown begins: 10-9-8...2-1! The SCMM 2014 has officially begun!

Groups A and B head out. We follow after at three-minute delay and we run. We run like a herd of cattle that has been let loose after being imprisoned for a year. We are finally on our way, eager to show the world what we are made of.

Race day wakes me up. It reminds me that I can train till I know the roads like the back of my hand, but at some point I have to go for it. For real.

As we begin to run, the strains of the national anthem are in the air and a lump wells up in my throat. It is an emotional moment. This is the culmination of our efforts of over six months to a year, a year of purely self-inflicted pain and hardship. All that sweat and anguish has come down to these few hours.

This is the end of the road, whatever the result; I head out into the unknown, filled with faith in myself and in my training.

Yes, even though this is my third marathon, it still feels like I am running into the unknown, because each race is different, just as each day is different. Most importantly, I am a different person. I am a year older with experiences that changed me.

It is a glorious day and I feel invincible.
I am running with faith that I can make it happen and with confidence that it is my day.
With the belief that I can do it.
I will do it.

"'Who are YOU?' said the Caterpillar.

This was not an encouraging opening for a conversation. Alice replied, 'I — I hardly know, sir, just at present — at least I know who I WAS when I got up this morning, but I think I must have been changed several times since then.'

'What do you mean by that?' said the Caterpillar sternly. 'Explain yourself!'

'I can't explain myself, I'm afraid, sir,' said Alice, 'because I'm not myself you see.'"

1

THE START

SCMM 2014: 5.43 am

And we are off! The race strategy was worked out well in advance. An easy warm up followed by a constant pace through the race, with a little slowing down on the inclines. Rohan, Vishal and I start well. We stay together, running bang on at our target pace. We run through Churchgate onto Marine Drive and head towards Nariman Point. We use a couple of these initial kilometres to warm up, starting at 6.45 minutes per km, and gradually working our way up to 6.15 minutes per km until we complete 4km. We finally settle into a race pace of 5.45 minutes per km. As I know well, it is crucial that we control our pace the in the beginning. I have previously paid the price of racing in the first few minutes.

When I started running in 2003, it was the most convenient form of exercise. I didn't need a gym membership, fancy clothes or gear.

I didn't need to go anywhere! I would just put on my old tracks, slip into my sports shoes and step out. All I had to do on any given morning was to look left and right and decide which way my heart would take me. On my left, 15 minutes down, was Marine Drive and on the right was Worli: both beautiful roads, with the sea awaiting me.

How much I ran depended on my schedule, which in turn depended on when my kids had to leave and what their plan was. On days when I ran late, after they left by the school bus, I ran along tree-lined Nepean Sea Road, a quaint neighbourhood with gentle rolling streets and hundred-year-old bungalows that is now being redeveloped into monstrous, modern, ultra-luxurious residences. These morning runs were simple, so simple that they just became part of my life. The more I ran, the better I felt. I began to see my morning runs as "my time", precious moments that I carved out more and more of, from my so-called busy life. Each time I headed out, I found myself leaving behind my mental baggage.

The very act of running is a liberating one. The wind against my face, blood rushing to my brain, my rhythmic heartbeat, hair flying in the breeze, smiles of the other morning people and music in my ears. When I return home my whole demeanour is different. All the jumbled thoughts in my head would clear up as I pound the street, sometimes hard, sometimes soft, with my thoughts coming sometimes fast and sometimes slow, or sometimes none at all, keeping time with the pace of my run. I come home energized, ready to face the humdrum upon the wings of my runner's high.

I realised that the time we spend running is our quiet time. It is the time we use for introspection. During this time we reach within and renew ourselves for real life, equipping ourselves to deal with the real world. We use this to make our spirit whole again, rejuvenate ourselves and heal our souls. This time is akin to the time people used to spend cooking, cleaning, sewing and tinkering with machines fifty years ago, activities that were mechanical and repetitive and allowed our brains to relax and calm down. Today, many of us don't have any of these prosaic activities as part of our daily routines. Running can replace these monotonous hobbies as a calming part of our day. Even though we may be running with people, at some point during the run we connect with ourselves, and subconsciously resolve our internal conflicts. Under the banality of putting one foot in front of the other, what happens is a complex process of self-actualisation, which eventually makes each of us better people, better parents, better children and better friends. The shackles of the world we have around us need to be shed before the true self can emerge.

Nearly 10 years have passed since I discovered the therapeutic power of running. Much has changed. I feel I have now graduated as a runner. From being a "happy" runner I have become one of those who train towards a goal. The one thing that hasn't changed is that running still teaches me things about myself as I break through each layer of life experiences and see myself with greater clarity. The time I spend running is like walking the conceptual path, which is thought to lead to the true nature of reality. Infinitesimally deep and complex.

Running was the key to my life falling into place again after it was turned upside down. The more I ran, the more confidence I gained, the happier I became. I gathered enough courage to start work. Getting back to design was a rewarding experience and with the kids, school work and a home to run, my plate seemed full. Most importantly, running fuelled my writing and my blog was born.

Do I write because I run? Yes.
Am I the person I am because I run? Yes.
Running lifts the fog from my brain.

We find a million excuses not to do things for ourselves. Guilt is a big factor in our lives, just waiting to rein in our desires. We runners balance a lot. Work. Spouses. Kids. Homes. Friends. Real life. Running allows you to do all that and squeeze more out of life. What's more, it's a great way to get out of a rut. One of my favourite lines is "You are only one run away from good mood!" I am a firm believer in this and many a time when I have been irritable my kids tell me, "Mom, you should go for a run!"

When I finished my first half marathon in all of 2 hours and 45 minutes at SCMM 2005, I felt like I had accomplished a huge thing, even though I walked a lot of the last 4-5km. That didn't matter. My time didn't matter. Going the whole distance was an achievement in itself.

As a child I had resisted learning the keyboard, but when my children started learning to play it, I realised that the sound of music was soothing. The discipline and focus that I needed in order to play a piece correctly trained my brain to live in the moment. Their music teacher became mine too as I started learning to play the keyboard with them, taking three Trinity Grade exams over the next three years.

I failed the last one, much to my chagrin. Not to be deterred by this, after one year I was at it again, only now I moved to playing the piano! Starting at the beginners' level and moving up to the intermediate level was a fulfilling experience. What comes to my children so easily has been quite a struggle for me. But I keep at it, with determination, week after week, moving the bar up slowly, but steadily.

Learning new things and having varied experiences are what matter, whether or not we succeed or fail at these. Having the courage to try something new is a kind of success in itself.

From 2003, when I first started running, until September 2009, I ran by myself. I had registered for the inaugural 2004 SCMM but I did not run it. Since 2005, I have run all the Mumbai half marathons until 2011. I ran because I had just discovered the joy of running. I was happy to simply train and train and train and train with no set goal in mind and no race day marked on my calendar. Six years of erratic running. I did shave off a few minutes of my time with each successive race. The turning point came when I was introduced to Savio D'souza by my friend Nimisha. Savio is India's greatest marathoner and his group is called Savio's Stars.

Nimisha had been in school with my sister. I remember her cheering me on at the half marathons. One day in 2008, she called me and said "Parul, I want to run too." That was when she started training with Savio. What a beautiful feeling it was, to see that she was inspired by me! Nothing like it had ever happened to me before.

I have seen the SCMM grow five-fold from a small race of 3,000 half marathoners and 800 marathoners in 2004 to a crowd of 15,000 jostling each other on the sea link, to a group of 3,500 marathoners at the start line in 2014. This event has changed the lifestyle of Indians, who are essentially a lazy lot, made them give up their Sunday morning sleep and develop healthy food habits. Instead of going out and drinking and partying on Saturday nights, the Sunday morning run has become a more refreshing option!

The marathon is a charismatic event. It has everything. It has drama. It has competition. It has camaraderie. It has heroism. No other sport has so many competitors at the same time. I was surrounded by people and yet I was one with myself. Reflecting. Thinking. Constantly talking to myself to overcome my own anxieties. Even within the crowd I was alone.

When I started running with the group, I met Vishal, who also lived in the same vicinity as Nimisha and I. We ran at the same pace, always trained together and went together, as Vishal, the perfect gentleman, insisted on picking us up every single time. I joined them tentatively, wondering how I would fit this regimented schedule into my complicated life, a life in which I largely had to keep other people's schedules. At that point, everybody else's agenda seemed more important than mine, especially my kids'.

Monday recovery runs began at 6 am at Nariman Point, Wednesdays, we met at Priyadarshini Park at 6 am, and Fridays at Nariman Point again, followed by the long run on Sundays. Some people also went on Tuesdays and Thursdays for strength training and stretching! I thought I would never see my kids off to school if I did this. One month with the group and my horizon expanded. I saw the world in a different way. I managed to work out a schedule that would balance both.

Running with a group, guided by a coach, changed the game for me completely. This motley group had a common passion, bordering on madness. Here, I met people who trained hard for half marathons, marathons as well as for ultra marathons. Some who were extremely busy and several who did many other activities besides running, but all made the time to run. The more I interacted with them, the more I realized that these people loved to challenge themselves and create new boundaries.

Learning from them, I pushed my limits with time and distance and discovered a new way to live. Emulating them, I wanted to move out of my comfort zone. As I fell into the routine I imbibed a lot. The warmth of conversation mitigated the pain of the tough workouts. Running with so many people, I lost the sense of how well or poorly I ran. I just went with the flow, the rhythm of our footsteps and the steady breathing. I was sharing something. I was a part of something larger. We were a pack who ran as one. Not really competing with anyone, let alone each other.

November 2010, Delhi
My first out-of-town run

Within two months of joining the group, here I was with them, away from the known and familiar, in Delhi, to run a fast 21km race. My excitement knew no bounds. Seeing a city on my feet during a run allowed me to capture the pulse of the place.

However, the highlight of this trip turned out to be the food. Dinner! Breakfast! Lunch! Indian! Pasta! Veg! Non-veg! It was hilarious, how fanatical we runners could be about our meals! We spent two days together and were a part of gruelling event, and this created quite a bond. Some of us experienced knee pain, cramping and general exhaustion, whereas the others were fresh. We raced together and suffered the aftermath, and this united us.

The run itself was fantastic. It began at 7.30am, which was incredibly late for us Mumbaikars, but even at that hour Delhi was cold. I layered up, but that turned out to be unnecessary as the buzz kept me warm. We were witnessed only by a small crowd, as I believe that Delhiites are a lethargic bunch. We began with a bang, with the three of us – Nimisha, Vishal and I – keeping pace. We breezed along until I hit the panic button and thought that the pace was too fast for me. I let the others get ahead while I enjoyed the shady avenues, the beautiful stretch alongside India Gate and the backdrop of Rashtrapati Bhavan. The route was flat, with only one small incline. As I approached the 15km mark, I realized I was not tired at all. I decided to step it up, and at 16km I was in full flow. It went on like this until the end, when I sprinted towards the finish.

It was an exhilarating finish and my best ever! I clocked 2:17:24 and was really happy with this timing. I had enjoyed myself immensely, especially the challenge of running in new terrain. What was even better was the knowledge that I had achieved my best time without even pushing myself that hard. If this was the case, how much further then could I go when I put my heart and soul into a run?

My closest friend Sukhpreet ran the Pondicherry 10km in 2011, only to accompany me during my half marathon. She was soon addicted. Since then, she has not missed a single Mumbai or Delhi half marathon. Most people I meet ask me why I run. Several other friends and acquaintances call me to ask how they can start running too. I love talking about it. I tell them to try it for a few weeks and see how it great it makes them feel. (I don't tell them that it will soon become their life!) I am happiest when I can inspire non-runners to take it up as a hobby.

Here's what I usually tell them:

1. Start small. Run 5km.
2. Walk and run if you have to, but complete the distance you have set out to do.
3. With each run you will get stronger and you will see the difference in a couple of months.
4. Pick up the pace. Run 10km. Keep it easy. Keep it fun. Don't be in a hurry.
5. Patience. Patience. Patience.
6. Fitness, distance and speed will come in due course, with hard work and regularity.
7. Push yourself. Run 15km. Set goals. Realistic goals. Gather confidence. Once these targets are met you can easily move ahead.
8. Become brave. Run 18km. Go for it. Want more. Get ready to

give more time, more effort.

9. As you mature as a person and a runner, run 21km. The target will seem more achievable simply because you have changed.

10. Enjoy it. Live it. Love it. Realise that once you commit to it, nothing is impossible

February 2011, Pondicherry
One month after my decision to run my first full marathon

The motto of the race was: Joy of Running. As we reached the holding area, we were welcomed by a booming Frenchman announcing that race would just begin at 5.30am under the starlit sky. As minutes of the cold early morning ticked by, we were roused out of our lethargy by a pop song from the eighties. A local French aerobics instructor was demonstrating a warm up routine. The 300-odd half marathoners followed the Jane Fonda-esque routine. At the end of 15 minutes of warm up, there were smiles all around and the entire mob loosened up.

Pondicherry was a unique trail run. Each turn along the route framed a new vista. Parts of it were rocky, some were paved and others long patches of sand. There were also a couple of cattle traps which served as few moments of rest. Along the run we heard several bird calls, and in the clearing on the side I even chanced upon a peacock.

By daybreak, I reached the 6km mark and I saw 2 of my friends, Kochi and Ashwin, both superfast runners, returning. I wondered if they were so fast that they had looped me already or whether I was really that slow! A few minutes later, they crossed us again.

They had run out too fast in the dark and as a result gone off the trail. All in all, in this race, instead of 21km they ran 26km!

After we completed our half marathon, we waited for the full marathoners to finish. They served us a hot South Indian breakfast (no spoons, only fingers!). The simplicity of the event reflected the philosophy and mindset of Auroville, the city of dawn, an experimental township that is two hours away from Chennai. The ashram itself emanated peace and I felt one with nature.

We celebrated the run with friends over dinner. With mirth and merriment we sat around and talked of nothing. As we walked back to our hotel at midnight under a sky of stars, I realized this was a day I would never forget. I had been introduced to Sri Aurobindo, run a trail run that was permanently imprinted on my mind and had just had a memorable night. The miracle of magic was complete.

There have been several more runs: on vacation in Thailand, I ran a 10km race along the beach to save turtles (in which I stood fourth!). There was another in Cubbon Park, Bangalore, a 10km trail on one of my work trips. And of course the Capitol Hill 10km race, around Washington D.C.'s most historic neighbourhood.

Each of these experiences has been amazing. Each run has been unique. The friends that I have made have become family. There is great camaraderie in running a marathon, because amidst song, conversation and shared pain, we have forged many a new bond. There is a reason we love to run, there is a reason, timeless and true, why we seek each other, why we work so hard, why we search for the best path, why we challenge and inspire each other, why we seek hills and practice acts of endurance. We are training and it matters more than we understand. We have mutual respect and admiration for one another. We understand the level of pain that we must endure. We don't question each other about why we continue to test ourselves in this way. We simply accept that we each have our reasons. Running has helped us find ourselves in some way, has helped us understand ourselves better.

Every runner has a story.
Here is mine.

The universal truth:
Kabir ke dohe
Meerabai's songs
Shakespeare's plays
Shelley's poems.

Different genres
Distinct eras
Varied tongues
All great.

What philosophers teach
And religions preach,
All saying the same thing
Essentially teaching us the way to live.

The effervescence of love
About the fluidity of time
The cyclical nature of life
The only definitive – the End.

2

THE STORY

I grew up in a picture perfect world. Like all of us. Like most people we know. A secure, happy childhood, a rebellious adolescence and fun-filled twenties. We were one big Indian joint family: wonderful parents and a supporting close-knit extended family, all living together with grandparents, aunts and uncles, and pesky young cousins. It was an Ekta Kapoor primetime television show!

My school days whizzed past in a happy haze. The college years were my growing up years. After two years in junior college, I began studying architecture. This is when I got some exposure to the real world; I met people from various backgrounds and communities. My ivory tower had shielded me from it all!

But, before I could really get a taste of life, I met Ketu and fell in love.

It was a kind of love-arranged marriage. He wooed me for a couple of months and then, on a beautiful rainy evening he proposed to me at Worli Seaface, with Air Supply playing in the background.

We had a fairytale wedding and a happy marriage. The honeymoon lasted a long time.

Life seemed to be going as planned. After three years came Arnav. Ketu's love for him grew alongside his love for cars, cricket and expensive toys (the ridiculous snooker table and the mini golf set were prime examples). Three years later, Sanjana came along and became the apple of his eye. She was the only one who could make him do things which were very uncharacteristic of him! We were a "normal" family leading a "normal" life: work, gym, Saturday nights with friends, and the occasional fights.

In December 2002, we went on a small vacation to the nearby hill station of Mahabaleshwar. It was a simple holiday. We spent our days riding horses, going boating and eating a lot of good food.

Strawberries. Corn. Table Land with the crazy rides. It was a relaxing, idyllic trip.

While we were there, Ketu decided to visit the hotel's Ayurvedic centre for a massage. He consulted with the "Ayurvedic doctor" at the centre about his constipation problem. The "doctor" promptly prescribed "some pills" for Ketu to take.

By some unfathomable bad luck, Ketu took these pills religiously, and because I didn't know any better, I encouraged him to take them. Six months of prolonged ingestion resulted in high blood pressure, loss of hair and general fatigue. We attributed these symptoms to "Bombay Stress". We ignored all the warning signs and when we finally visited a doctor, it was too late. Ketu was diagnosed with acute kidney failure. The pills that he had been taking were laden with heavy metals, as was proved later by laboratory tests. But the damage had already been done. Our happy getaway had turned out to be a fatal trip. After months of hospitalisation and some major complications, the dark dawn of 8th September 2003 came upon us.

Ketu was no more. He was 35.

The glue that was holding our lives gave way and everything fell apart. For my family, my children, me.

We were lost. Broken. Devastated.

No path. No light. Only darkness.

The view from my window was exactly the same as it had been forever: the blue sky, grey sea, green grass and the birds chirping.

All the same, except for one small change. We had lost someone we loved. Forever. Ever and ever. I learnt what the word death really means. No words could console us.

Hours melted into days. Days into months. Time passed by but life was at a standstill.

The support we received from friends and family was overwhelming and unflinching, but who could put the pieces back together? Advice came from far and wide. This will pass, it will hurt less. Time will fill the void in my life.

The emptiness of the present was filled with things I had to do, day after day. I trudged through every hour of every day with bits and pieces of things I did. I could not fathom my new reality. I had always been someone who liked being prepared, whether what I was facing was an exam or throwing a small party. I liked knowing what I was getting into and understanding the rules. Now, I found myself confronted with a scenario for which I certainly wasn't prepared, let alone able to comprehend. No books. No sample papers. There was nothing to help me here.

For a long time, I grappled with self doubt. Wrestled the demons of anger. Loneliness. Insecurity. They still visit me sometimes!

How would I bring up my two children? How would I protect them? Guide them? What would happen to me? How would I face the world all by myself? There were questions from all sides and questions within me, but no answers. Not within me. Not from anyone. Just as our family and our well-wishers wondered how I would cope, I wondered the same thing. I had to allay my children's fears as well as mine.

Within a month of Ketu's demise, I attended Arnav's Open Day at his school. With trembling legs, I walked into his class and found a lot of couples alongside with several single parents. Seeing them was heartening, as I realised that so many of them had come alone too. Like me. I saw how they had come by themselves because their spouses were travelling, or living apart for work reasons. A lot of people were leading the "single lifestyle." Divorced people. Reality dawned on me. I was not the only one.

Slowly, I began to reconcile myself to my life. I accepted facts. Understood the new structure. The dynamic nature of life. The much repeated adage of change being the only constant became a reality for me.

So I took a deep breath and put my "situation" behind me. I went along with things as if all was "normal". In my reality this was normal. This was the only way it was going to be. With a smile camouflaging the anguish I felt, I participated in the Parents' Race on Sports Day. As a proud mother, I fought back tears as I saw my children on stage. I applauded them for their achievements, in the classroom and outside.

In the beginning, I had looked around me and seen no direction. Not knowing what to do did not stop me from trying to do. Things. Anything. Something. I started with just getting through my day-to-day activities. In retrospect, that was the correct way. To deal with something major, start by doing what is immediate. The bigger answers will come with time. Anyway, as I fell into a simple domestic routine, the children's school, extracurricular activities and my domestic chores, I felt something settling. I found purpose. I knew I had to claw my way out of this well, even though I could not see either grips or footholds ahead of me.

When we fall in life, we need a web of safety. The strength of this web is essential for survival. A strong web can be made of several strands, with the strength coming from the sheer volume of strands, or it can be made of very few strands, but extremely tensile ones. When one of the strands breaks, the web needs to modify itself so as to cover the loophole. My entire web was in tatters and I had to rebuild it slowly, strand by strand.

What could I do?

With my father-in-law's support, I started understanding the financials. With the love from my dear friends Ashish and Poorvi and their children, we filled our days with activities. And all the others, so many others, comforted us with their presence and phone calls.

We may think that people support us, but the props can only help you if you are strong enough to stand. A support system remains merely that, until there is motivation to move forward from within. This framework keeps you with the flow, but when you hit the eddies, it is the power from within which enables you to break out of the current and escape it. If something had to change in my life, I had to be the one to change it. There is no magic wand. And no one can do for you what you can do for yourself.

I was alone. We were alone.
This realization was devastating. But I had to do what I had to do.

The rose-tinted glasses of the past were shattered. Naked truth lay bare in front of me. It was like taking baby steps in a swimming pool. Venturing out into a new land with alien landscape. New boundaries were drawn up. I started to rebuild a new web from the fragments of my old one. The picture that emerged was nowhere close to the original. It was a new one, but was a complete one. With no cracks.
Our diminished unit of three — Arnav, Sanjana and me — had to become stronger than ever to withstand the vagaries of life. We

learnt to smile again. Find joy even in our incompleteness. We took holidays. With our friends, our family and even by ourselves. Small trips, big trips. These were scary at first. We started with Goa, close by and safe. Then, as the kids got older and I got braver, we ventured further out. Celebrated birthdays. As life would have it, Arnav shared his birthday with Ketu. So in a way, we silently celebrated Ketu along with Arnav. Festivals. Diwali had been the occasion of a customary party that Ketu and I used to throw for our friends. Only now I hosted it myself. Occasions. Report cards. Successes. Mothers' Day. New Year's Day. And the failures. Maths marks. Physics tests. Heartaches. We learnt to stand on our own feet and slowly, to walk again. Instead of coping with life, we began to live our lives. The pain of absence has been converted into the joy of remembrance. A celebration of what was!

Over time I have learned to look at things differently, I have learned to do new things and to do the old things in new ways. This is probably my period for evolution. My time to become a new person. To do things I had never imagined I would have done, or was capable of doing.
I had taken a deep breath, gathered courage and adapted into this new space, got myself acquainted with the geography. This was my new world. With the support of our family and friends, and a wonderful therapist, I found myself. I recognized the person I was. I opened my eyes to see the world.

A song from Sanjana's playlist by Kelly Clarkson sums it up well:
"What doesn't kill you only makes you stronger"

Life throws up the most unexpected ordeals. All of us have our own hells. Some self-created. Some situational. We have to just deal with it. Keep courage and have faith. Not get bogged down. Not allow our fears to get the better of us. That things will get better. They have to get better. Eventually. Maybe not soon enough. But sure enough, they do.

Ketu and I started a journey, and today, the kids and I have travelled along a path we chose. He has been a guiding force for us at all the significant junctions in our lives, and the decisions which I thought were unilateral have not been so in reality. The nine years we spent together have been a big influence in my life.

Ketu was a loving father, a sensitive husband and an intelligent man. He had a real bond with most of the people in his life. He had strong views and was not afraid to voice them. When he said something, he stood by it and propagated it, however radical. Ketu's conviction gave him the strength to think ahead of his time. He lived his life to the fullest and believed in dying young, like his idols Jim Morrison and Kurt Cobain. Maybe he was intuitive about his destiny.
I hope he is at peace wherever he is.
Cheers to Ketu. Cheers to life!

> *It is foolish and wrong to mourn the men who died.*
> *Rather we should thank God that such men lived.*
> *George Patton*

When I wake up in the morning it feels like a good morning and I look forward to the day. A day full of ups and downs, a day packed with work and errands, with kids and cooking. Everyday things.
But in between all this, we need to find time (perhaps not consciously) to feel good about ourselves, as we smile at a stranger, do a good deed, and feel content.

Meeting a long lost friend and talking about where I am today helps me reflect on my current place in the world. That is when I say, yes, things are great, and I look at all of life's faces, some good, some bad, but all accepted. We need moments of introspection to bring this realization into a part of our everyday being.

I hope that I will always be able to sleep in peace, looking forward to another daybreak, the pink of dawn turning into a full blown sunny day with all its joys and sorrows. I am happy with where I am today.
Being happy doesn't mean that everything is perfect. It means that you have decided to look beyond the imperfections.

3

FRAILTY AND STRENGTH

SCMM 2014: 2km.

Today, on the 17th of January, 2014, I have fought the demons of doubt and convinced myself that I am capable of doing this. Nothing can faze me!

We approach Nariman Point. Here we have spent many a Sunday morning engaged in post-run chitchat. Here we have lingered, long after the runs were over. Unsolicited advice, real running tips, words of encouragement, plans for future runs, and oh, even match-making, it has all happened here. I remember Savio's words from three years ago, on a Sunday like this: develop patience, he had said. Running the full marathon requires endurance, for which you will have to run much slower. Maverick speed will not get you anywhere. For any building to stand tall, he told me, it needs a strong foundation. I saw the truth in that. It was the same point I remembered hearing in one of the first lectures we had in our building construction class when I was studying architecture! More than immature and enthusiastic bursts of speed, we needed mature, sedate perseverance.

Among all the other things it can be, running is definitely time-consuming. On average, to put in weekly mileage of 50-60km, we need up to 10 waking hours (not necessarily daylight hours, as there have been a few times when we have started running at 4.30am too). Warm up; cool down, stretch, and yes, the post-run chitchat. A short run can take up 1.5 hours. And come Sunday, the day of our long run, it could take up to 4 or 4.5 hours, depending on the distance and the amount of time we spend dissecting the run or having breakfast. The reward for our labour!

The discipline of the 5 o' clock daily wake up alarm is a blessing. I fall asleep by 10pm on most days. Irrespective of whether I'm watching the most exciting part of a movie or having a really stimulating conversation, come 9.45pm, my eyes just close and I am in la-la land. Thus, my social timetable is completely reversed. Instead of meeting my friends for dinner or a late night movie, we catch up over breakfast.

To be able to dedicate this kind of time to a hobby (although I don't think running qualifies as that any more, since it has become a way of life for me) requires a lot of planning. Everything for the next day needs to be kept ready the day before: my work bag, kids' alarms and snack boxes, meals and the once-in-a-while school notice that requires a parent's signature. Due to the hot Mumbai weather, I usually start running between 5.15-5.30am depending on the distance, so that I am back in time. A sweaty red faced mom in shorts, with a wet pony tail, arriving in time to say good bye to her neat and well groomed, uniformed kids who are just boarding their school bus! Sometimes when, due to a miscalculation, I think I can't make it back on time, it acts as a spur and makes me run faster. Immediately after the kids leave, it is time for a quick shower and breakfast. I head out for work by 9.00-9.15am. The days I don't run, I do strength training at home. Core. General Strength. Legs. Upper body and abs.

On Wednesdays, when I run with the group, we finish by 7.45 or 8am and my kids don't see me at all. My running life has taught them to value my time. They know that when mom is out for a run, she is not reachable because I run without my cell phone. So we still leave notes for each other the old fashioned way on the bathroom mirror! Over the years, they have become self-reliant and responsible. They know that whatever they need from me for school needs to be taken the night before, or they will need to get it themselves, as I will be gone in the morning before they wake up. I have observed that they never miss the bus on Wednesdays. But on the other days, when they know I am around, their alarm is snoozed and there is utter chaos: socks are lost, forms are to be filled in at the last minute, and school books need to be gathered. The whole house is running helter-skelter trying to get them out by 7.20am. Banana and almonds in hand, shoelaces being tied in the lift, huffing and puffing, we make it to the bus. I wonder how they manage on other days!

In my mania to have it all, I have become a Master Multitasker. I have forgotten how to relax. I text while I walk and I talk on the phone while I'm on the road. I am constantly making lists, mental ones when I am running, and on paper when I am at a desk. Everything has to happen according to a plan. God forbid one thing goes haywire, and the whole schedule goes awry. A sick child. An emergency at work. And the life that I have carefully balanced spins out of control.

However, I am lucky that my work allows me the flexibility to make my own schedule and work from home. Over time, I have learnt to prioritize. Depending on the time of the year, different aspects become more important. Exams, holidays and my marathons determine my work and training schedule.

The key here is to recognise which issue is more demanding than the others, making it harder to handle. To manage it successfully requires more effort. To make my complicated life even more so, sometimes, I tend to add random activities to my existing lot, like organising a charity run, making t-shirts for the group or planning a post-run celebration. I even found the time every week to meet Ms. Patel, an old English teacher, to discuss philosophy and read the classics with. Having so much happening all the time makes the juggling even trickier, but it definitely makes life more satisfying!

Time management is an important skill. Living by clockwork, we can manage our hectic schedules. We can fulfil all our life's responsibilities and still carve out key blocks of time which we need for training. We should focus on what is important now and the rest will fall in place.

Needless to say, along with the days when things roll along smoothly, there have been several days when my kids have not taken the money to school that they had to, or not worn the correct clothes. Because I forgot to tell them. Because I was not there. Handling all this becomes a bigger challenge on days when things are not routine. Exams. Extra-curriculars. Open days. Assemblies. Half-days. On those days, I run either ridiculously early, or ridiculously late, after 7.30am. Managing all this is not just 'not easy'. It is very hard.

There have been enough moments when I feel I need to stop the world from turning, as it is spinning too fast and I can't cope. Temporarily, everything seems like it is one big jumble. On those days, I stumble through life. Once I realise where I am, I slowly begin to gather my focus again. Over time, I have developed coping mechanisms. Some 'me time'. A couple of runs. Heart to hearts with my inner circle.Lunch with the girls. Shopping. Crying in the bathroom. And then, I am ready to take on the world again.

I do all this and more because I want to. Over several years, my recovery period has shortened. I have learnt that the feelings I have now, a part of my "down phase", cannot last forever.
This too, shall pass, and all will be well again. I need to run through it. Let time pass by. Let life pass by.

When I would return home, Sanjana is waiting to ask me how much I ran. As I graduated from running the half marathon to the full marathon, her reaction to my distances has also changed. Now when I tell her, I did 18k she says, "Oh! Only?" and we laugh.

On and off, the insecurity of being a single parent makes me come down a little hard on my children. I try doubly hard to be both a role-model and a "perfect" parent. I have to play the good cop and the bad cop. Sometimes, I forget to have fun along the way.

Am I tiger mom? Yes, perhaps. Maybe I don't know any better, but I am willing to learn. I have learnt the realities of life the hard way. Maybe that has hardened me. But, I am on the path to softening my heart again. After years of being Ms. Invincible, I am discovering the beauty of vulnerability.

The face I show to the world is the "all is cool" face. I think it is important for me to maintain that façade and not show that I am human and sensitive and that I too feel pain. Tiny things, like a form on which I have to put in my marital status, or a song from the past, can crack the veneer of courage and plunge me back into the dark depths of despair.

The fact is that we all have weaknesses. Flaws. That is what reality is. That is what life is about. We need to recognise those facets of ourselves and accept them. Accept them and try to deal with them. Some we can change right away. Others take time and effort. So let us learn to live with them and make the best of our circumstances. .

September 2013: Sunday long run
Training for my third marathon.

With much pomp and grandeur the monsoon bid us adieu. Since then, the temperature and humidity rose steadily, along with the kilometres. I was now working on negative splits, increasing my speed believing that if I did so, the stamina for mileage would come. With two full marathons below my belt, I wanted to up my speed along with my endurance. To do this, I was running relatively shorter distances at faster paces.

I ran the first half at a regular long run pace, and stepped it up in the last 5-6km. It took a lot of determination to move my tired legs and to push my drained brain. It consumed my entire being to keep going. But I stuck at it, with only one single thought, that I should keep going, and that this too would end.

That day, I ran 18km. Last four of those kilometres were run at 5.33km per minute. I got a stitch at this speed and I wanted to give up. I actually stopped for two seconds, but started running immediately after. I ran with the pain because I wanted to. I ran because I could and focused all my energy towards the one goal I had today. I did it. I felt I had died. But, died and gone to heaven!

At the end of the run, I overheard some of the other runners discussing the humidity. I had not even noticed! Me, whose favourite peeve is the weather, the sun, the temperature! I just ran. It was only me and the road. I was reminded of a quote from Kristen Armstrong's blog: "What you focus on expands." It sparked an epiphany. I now understood what had been going on in my brain. I had spent so much time focusing on the difficulties, the weather, the distance, et al. which only made the run harder. The mere thought of what is to come becomes all-consuming and much bigger than the actual challenge. The trick then, was to master the mind. This is not just applicable to running, but to any issue or crisis that seems overwhelming in life.

Life rules apply to running.
Running rules apply to life.

> *Running is a metaphor for life.*
> *Oprah Winfrey, when she ran her marathon.*

I ran through summer.
I ran on days I didn't really want to run on.
I completed the distance I set out to.
I kept at it even though I knew I was out of form.
My training continues.
It has become a habit.
It is not an afterthought.
The training is a part of my integral routine.
I look forward to days when I will breeze through my run.
But I also know that every day cannot be my day.
I am happy to persevere.

4

REBIRTH

SCMM 2014: 3km.

Running along Marine Drive is always a pleasure. Marine Drive is a 3km long, six-lane concrete road in southern Mumbai which stretches north along the coastline, forming a natural bay in the Arabian Sea. This C-shaped road links Nariman Point to Babulnath. Art deco buildings line the entire seafront, making it one the most exciting skylines in the world. Affectionately referred to as The Queen's Necklace because of its row of sparkling lights at night time, it is a place that can be whatever you want it to be. You can go there alone to reflect on life against the serene setting of the setting sun and crashing waves. Or you can hang out with a bunch of people and talk about silly nothings and while away your time. The scenic beauty of the perfectly aligned palm trees with the sea beyond offers an enthralling experience.

From here on, until we head onto the sea link, it is our territory. Familiar territory. We know each curve, each bump, and the changing vista has been imprinted in our minds, has almost become a part of the subconscious. I own this. Vishal, Rohan and I have now settled into our rhythm. We chat merrily along the way, as if it were like just another long run. However, my refrain at every kilometre is "Don't make me talk! I don't have any extra energy to expend on this inane conversation!" Despite this, my chatter continues.

Running along this route stirs up nostalgia. Although the road is packed with runners today, my most memorable trip here was when it was deserted.

July 19, 2011:
The height of the monsoon

As I picked up a drowsy Nimisha, she said, "But, Parul, it's raining!"

I looked around and agreed, as I realized that it had been pouring all night. After much deliberation, we drove slowly to Nariman Point, wondering if any of the others would show up.

Lo and behold, almost everyone was there despite the incessant rain. It wasn't just a drizzle that showed signs of letting up either. No sir, it was a proper downpour! Under cover of the dark shadow cast by the clouds, we all trooped out in batches, with most of us attempting our longest runs of the season.

3-4km into the run, the rain grew heavier. We were drenched to the bone. The rain fell in large drops and we couldn't keep our eyes open in the deluge. The pitter-patter of our feet matched the rhythm of the falling raindrops.

People often ask us, whether we run during the monsoon. I really can't understand the question. After we have suffered through the tropical heat of summer, the rainy season is a welcome relief. Besides, runners are like kids. I believe that running is a grownup's lost link to playing outside. We enjoy the feeling of freedom as we run, and during the monsoon there is the added pleasure of splashing through all the puddles! Plus, our skin is water proof, isn't it?

We ran along and passed a few runners who had all realized what a treat it was to be out running that day. We ran past a few early morning walkers who had braved the rain. Some had umbrellas, while others had windcheaters or raincoats. But there was one common thread linking them: the look of incredulity on their faces when they saw us. Are you crazy, they seemed to ask, and our response to this was a resounding yes! I wanted to say to them, "Ditch the umbrella and cleanse your soul!"

We finished the run with huge smiles as we completed the distance of a half marathon with ease. That morning run is tied in my mind to a quotation I saw on a fellow runner's t-shirt in Pondicherry: "I run, therefore I am nuts!"

Each raindrop reinforced our insanity.
Each raindrop etched this perfect morning in our memory.
This is what I live for.

I have learnt, that it is not possible (or I should say, it is very difficult) to have a perfect life. But life can be a collection of perfect moments. These can come at the most unexpected time, all we need to do is recognise them and capture them in our memories, and they become ours to treasure forever.

SCMM 2014: 5km.

The memory of our monsoon run makes Vishal, Rohan and I burst into laughter, and we cruise along until we reach the first of the hills. This is the Babulnath incline, which is not really a hill, but for me even a speed-breaker counts as one. Not so long ago, when I still ran half marathons, I used to call it my Mount Everest. It does not frighten me so much anymore. So we drop the pace slightly and continue over Peddar Road and then downhill.

This is where Vishal, Nimisha and I live. A residential area where most of our friends live too. An important arterial road in the geography of Mumbai. With mid-rise buildings lining both sides of this narrow road, this was where the biggest crowd of supporters gathered, though later in the day when we would be on our way back. Despite the early hour, my sister and our family friends, Pradeepkaka and Kokilakaki, make it a point every year to look for me in the pre-dawn darkness. I call out to the dear 70-year-old couple and carry on.

The race has just begun.
9km done.

We have warmed up well.
Our muscles are fresh.
These are the easy kilometres.

In the good old days, I used to run from traffic signal to traffic signal. 10km was 5 traffic signals along Marine Drive until Walkeshwar, a residential neighbourhood at the north-western end of the Marine Drive loop. Easy. Comfortable. For longer runs, I would go up to 15km. As I started training for the full marathon, I suddenly realised that these signals had lost the meaning they used to have for me. Today, a short run is 10km, a medium one is 18km and a long one is anything over 25km. While training, I unconsciously created new landmarks, which are a good 3 - 4km apart and cover 5 -7 traffic signals at least! 25 kilometres is now only a series of 5 roads: Marine Drive, Babulnath, Peddar Road, Haji Ali and Worli Seaface. Not such a long run!

I was amazed at how my perception of a long run had changed from 18km to 30km. I had broken up the distance into smaller (more doable) cutoffs, but even these were 3-4 times the distance that had I been running for the past so many years.

What used to be long had now become short. Everything in life is relative.

What seems to be a huge task is actually only a series of smaller milestones.

From a book I read by Dr. APJ Abdul Kalam:

"Dream Big.
Dream, Dream, Dream,
Dreams transform into thoughts
And thoughts result into action."

The longer I run the bigger my dreams become.

SCMM 2011
My last half marathon

It had been 3 years since I'd begun running the half marathon seriously. Each year, I would see the full marathoners run past me in the opposite direction, towards the half way point. I would cheer them and say, "Go, full marathoners go!" It took me a while to realise that 'full' was an unnecessary word: you are either a marathoner or you aren't. A half marathoner is a half marathoner. I knew then that one day in the near future, I would be with them, on the other side, their side, to complete my journey by becoming a marathoner.

Today, at kilometre 17, I rounded the curve at Babulnath and came onto Chowpatty. The view awaiting me was inspiring. Soft white clouds were set against a deep blue sky, with the sea glimmering against the deserted sand. It felt like I was seeing my city for the first time, but the sights, sounds and smells seemed so familiar. The beach. The sea. The Art Deco skyline. This, I thought, was the best

SAVIO'S STARS

SCMM 2013 - FLYING OVER THE SEALINK - VISHAL, PARUL, SUNIL, ROHAN

THE RISINGS- VISHAL, NIMISHA, PARUL

SCMM 2012 - MY FIRST FULL MARATHON

4TH PLACE IN A 10K RACE, PHUKET

SCMMM 2014 - RAINA PACING
ME TO THE FINISH

WITH THE LEGENDARY SAVIO D'SOUZA

SMILING SANJANA

HANDSOME ARNAV

AT LAKE TAPOLA, THE FATEFUL MAHABALESHWAR TRIP, 2002

HAPPY TIMES

THE ADVENTUROUS TRIO

SCMM 2013

4:09:22

SCMM 2014

MY FIRST EVER RACE IN 1976 - U.K.G.

city in the world. At that moment, I felt invincible. The endorphins had kicked in and I felt I could do anything in the world. Nothing was impossible. Crossing the finish line with my arms held out wide, I wondered if I was flying. I was! I was sprinting the last 50m of my 21.1km. 2:08 hours! What a high! It was a dream finish.

The moment of truth arrived: at the SCMM 2012, I would register for the full marathon.

But when Sunday evening approached, the enormity of my decision overwhelmed me. What was I thinking? A marathon is not only double the distance of a half marathon, it is at least three times as hard. Clearly, I wasn't thinking straight! As I told my story to my non-runner friend, she said, "It's your endorphins talking!"

Endorphins = morphine within. I was riding the high! These brain induced opiates had made me euphoric and my perception of pain was reduced. Scientifically, endorphins are produced during running and they attach themselves to the areas of the brain which are associated with emotions, the same areas that are activated when one experiences romantic love or while listening to music that sends a shiver down your spine, like Rachmaninoff's Concerto No. 3. The greater the endorphins in the brain, the more the euphoric you become. That is why runners are happy people. After most runs, one feels relaxed and clear headed, but it is these 2-hour runs that generate an extreme experience. I was experiencing a "Runner's High", when my mind took over my body and the unconscious led my mind.

The lesson in all this? Don't take any major decisions until after

2pm on Sundays when you have just completed a long run!
Anyway, the Three Musketeers – Vishal, Nimisha and I – were
committed to running the full marathon at the SCMM 2012.

We trained together with unwavering discipline. Suffered together.
We bonded over sweat and movie stories. Mehlam nicknamed our
trio "The Risings". We were the underdogs of the group and Savio
was the only one who believed in our ability. He had more faith in
us than we had in ourselves!

We did not stop running after our last half marathon in SCMM
2011. In February, we ran in Pondicherry, in March I did the DNA
women's run, and then I did the Thane half marathon. We kept at
it with single-minded determination. Doggedness became a part
of our vocabulary. The objective was to keep building mileage, and
hence endurance. There was no focus on time. This first marathon,
our goal was only to complete the distance.

2011 was a difficult year for me. After a prolonged illness, my father-
in-law passed away in October 2011. He had been our backbone,
radiating strength and support. He was open-minded and a visionary.
Being email savvy (he learnt how to use a computer at 70), he spent
a large part of his day sending motivational emails to all of us. They
became chain emails in a very short time: all his friends circulated
the same emails to each other! For me, he was a source of wisdom.
His kind words lifted me out my darkest moments.

When no one could see the path ahead, he shone the light and forged
ahead. Post-Ketu, it was his far-sightedness that rebuilt our family.

Putting his own loss behind him, he nurtured his grandchildren. With Arnav he was a football fan, keeping track of all the EPL games and cheering Chelsea on. With Sanjana, he listened to all her stories, and answered all her questions, however never-ending they felt! His death brought our family even closer together, as we now had to draw courage from each other. I had stopped running completely during his last days. After his death I could not muster up the will to go out again.

It was Vishal and Nimisha to the rescue again. They pulled me on the road one fine day, out of my inertia and that was it. I was back. Back to the routine. Back to what I loved doing.
With only two months left and January 2012 looming large, I needed to focus now. Out came the iPod to the rescue. I had given it up a few years ago, as I realized I didn't really need it. Most runners don't use music as it distracts the mind and takes away from the running. So I ran with my silence and my music on some days, and with the merry chatter of Nimisha and Vishal on the others.

Running helped me heal again. I learnt how to translate the emotional pain into physical pain. The repetitive, mind-numbing thumping of my feet helped me ruminate and untangle the thoughts in my muddled head. As my running became stronger, I let go of the pain more easily.

SCMM 2012
Day of reckoning

The group started with Nimisha, Vishal, Santa, Rohan, Ashish, Chaya and me. After the first few kilometres, I decided to run at a slower pace than the others, as I was not comfortable at their pace. So it was just Chaya and me, chugging along. We could see the others in the distance for a while, but they were soon gone.

Kilometres flew past and we ran over the sea link at dawn. Looking eastward we saw the sunrise over the Mumbai skyline. It was a spiritual moment. It occurred to me then that anybody can do just about anything that they really want to if they make up their mind to do it. We are capable of greater things than we realize.

Chaya and I chatted through the distance, finding others along the way to keep us company. We had crossed the halfway mark well on schedule: 2:17 hours for the first 21km! All we had to do was continue at this pace, and if we could push it just a little bit, we were headed for a sub 4:30 hour finish. A dream finish for our first marathon! Savio had predicted this time exactly a month ago, and we had laughed then. It just did not seem doable. But I see now...

As we rounded the corner at Mahim, I saw that my parents had come out to surprise me! That brought a huge smile to my face. All went well as we approached Worli, and both Chaya and I plugged in our iPods to step up our pace.

At kilometre 28, Nikita was waiting for me with my gel. I was in great spirits, and I waved to my parents again, who had reached the spot by then.

Only the home stretch remained: Worli, Peddar Road, Chowpatty and Churchgate!

We kept going. We walked a bit and ran a bit over Peddar Road, because of the incline. The high point came when I ran past my apartment building, where Arnav and Sanjana and my friends and family were out in full force cheering. A refreshing cool spray from Sanjana, and a chilled can of Coke from Arnav, opened and ready for me to down. After four sips, I was rejuvenated! The euphoria was short lived, as Sushant's words rang in my ears: after kilometre 32, the marathon begins. An experienced runner, he had warned me that the last 10km are the true test.

As I ran down towards Chowpatty and took the turn onto the main road. The sun shone on me in its full glory! Oh no! I was ready to give up then. The heat of the sun and the fatigue caught up with me. My legs were complaining and my brain was revolting.

Chaya had gone ahead and I was all by myself. I trotted along, looking for any excuse to stop. Painkiller spray on my non-existent pain, a water break and last of all, boredom! I had to kick myself to keep going. The 4:30 finish was within striking range. I kept making calculations in my head: last 5km at 6 minutes a kilometre and I could do it! After a few minutes, I had mixed up pace for time and it was all a jumble. That was when I decided to just leave it all behind and run. After the Marine Drive flyover, I met enough friends who helped me reach the finish.

At kilometre 41, I saw my friend Harish, waiting with his 9-year-old daughter, Raina. She was really excited to see me and ran a good

50m at her fastest speed. I struggled to keep up with her, but did it!

In my practice runs, I would sprint to the finish after struggling through the last few kilometres. Sure enough, it was the same on race day. Suvir, Savio and Sukhpreet were all waiting for me at the last 200m. It was a moment I'd never forget! The whole scene was surreal. It was an amazing realisation to know that I could pick up my feet and sprint and forget all my pain as I dashed to the finish, creating history.

All of us first timers clocked admirable times, ranging from 4:20 to 4:40 hours. For me, it was 4:35 hours.
A new phase in my life had begun.

With my father-in-law gone, we were really on own our now. I had to derive strength from his positive attitude towards life, just look ahead, and toughen myself up to shoulder all my responsibilities.

Instead of ruing what was gone, I focussed on what I had. Two wonderful children. An extremely supportive family and circle of friends. Thank god for them. This web of love broke the fall yet again. I regrouped and reinvented myself.

I had just run my first full marathon, Along with running, I discovered how to skip, scamper, spring, cavort, prance, frolic, romp, revel, ramble, hop, explore, wander, dash, dart, and delight.

As the rhythm picks up
And the world passes by
Each moment comes alive
Jostling for attention.

Flashes of humour
Sprinkled with sunshine
Wandering thoughts
Fluttering in the breeze
Hidden memories
Light up the face
And the smile surprises the onlooker!

As I look within
I find the answers I didn't know I was looking for.

5

ENDURANCE

SCMM 2014: 9km.

From Haji Ali to Mela, time flies. Haji Ali, both a mosque and a tomb built in 1431, sits right out in the ocean on your left, connected to land by a narrow pathway. The pathway is completely submerged during high tide, giving the impression that the mosque is floating on water. We greet the half marathoners on the other side, across the rows of tall dancing casuarinas and they cheer us on. I am sure a lot of them aspire to be on our side next year! We soon round the corner at Mela and reach Worli Sea face. It is a beautiful promenade with many residential buildings, which ensures a lot of crowd support.

Just before getting onto the sea link at kilometre 14, I discover that my iPod has fallen somewhere along the way, and the first of my demons returns. I will have to battle the slog kilometres by myself. I put that behind me within 5 minutes. There will be no negativity today. We joke that Rohan and Vishal will get me a new one as I am keeping pace with them at their personal best time. All is going as planned.

The sea link has a gentle incline, so we drop our pace a bit. To run on the sea link is a beautiful experience. The expanse and the sea make me feel like I am soaring. Vishal, Sunil, Rohan and I have a beautiful photograph on this bridge, from SCMM 2013, when all of us were airborne, having just completed 18km.

December 2004.
My most memorable 18km.

We were on a family vacation in New Zealand. Our cousins stayed about an hour outside of Auckland. I settled the kids for the afternoon with a movie and popcorn and left. It was a winding road along the sea. A beautiful road. Gently sloping down towards Auckland. It was 2pm when I started, a crisp day, with sunshine, fluffy clouds and playful waves. Trees lined most of the road, and flowers surprised me along the way. I ran light. I ran easy. I sang to myself. I stopped at the halfway mark to stretch. There was a rocky outcrop, so I caught the view. An expanse of the cerulean sky melting into the fresh blue sea, with the silvery playful waves beating against the pristine sand. Large white birds -- I think it was a colony of seagulls – were nestled in the hollow of the ivory cliffs. The grey rock contrasted with the fresh green tufts of shrubs. It was spellbinding. I just stood there in stunned silence trying to absorb the spectacle. The beauty seeped into me. I was one with nature. I was on a high.

And then in that moment my entire life came crashing down on me. I burst into tears. I was vulnerable. Exposed. My whole life flashed in front of me. The past. The present. I experienced a Runner's High for the first time.

The old wound had reopened. My loneliness engulfed me. The last 16 months had been a rollercoaster ride. The biggest and scariest one ever. But now, the ride was over and I could get off. The wall was cracking. My anger was escaping.

I accepted life. Accepted my destiny.

I was ready to forgive.

A few things died within me:
My pride.
My identity.
Expectations
The past.

I was ready to acknowledge the past, eulogize it and lay it to rest. I let my demons go, set them free, on scattered petals, on feathery wings, on helium towards the clouds.

On my way back I walked the steeper slopes. I had shed some of my burden along this road to Whangaparaoa. I began to run towards my future.
Unencumbered.
Forgiven
Free.

I began to know myself better.
Feel more.
Smile more.
Cry more.
I could see my flaws better, and I saw more good in others.
I felt the pain of others, and shared in their happiness too.
Each step that I took forward was taking me away from a past that I wanted to remember but not be held back by. I was running towards the portal to a new life. A new world.

January 2012.
The week after my first full marathon.

After the marathon, I had rested on my laurels. But there was also an incredible feeling of loss. I felt a void in my life due to the lack of a goal. Post-marathon depression is common, especially after the first one. Like any big event in life. After all the planning and the work is done, no matter what the result, you will feel a bit let down. I had spent one whole year planning for this day: eating, sleeping and dreaming of these 42.2km. And it was done!

Pushing my accomplishment out of my mind, I looked ahead. All I saw was the long road ahead with no real aim. The next year's marathon was too far away. Summer loomed ahead of me and there were no other runs planned. I could, of course, continue running, but that somehow was not enough motivation to get me out of bed in that prolonged Bombay winter. I was at a complete loss.

As the weather got warmer, I felt the urge to learn something new. I wanted to learn to swim! The breast stroke that I had learnt as a child was enough to save my life, but now I needed to use swimming as cross training to improve my running. To improve my lung capacity so I could run faster!

So there I was, bright and early on the day of the spring equinox, waiting at the club for the coach who had also trained my little fish, Sanjana. I was initiated into the technicalities step by step. Each step was apparently simple. The trouble began when, three weeks into the class, the coach told me to do them all simultaneously. To co-ordinate my breathing with the rhythm of my legs as well as maintain smooth arm motion was not only daunting, but impossible! I would invariably forget one or the other. The worst was when I forgot to breathe and went under. I came up sputtering, much to the amusement of the seasoned lady swimmer gliding past me!

While swimming, I forgot everything around me. I was in the moment to grasp the action. The joy of learning a new thing is what really stimulates the mind. As kids we constantly learnt new things. That is why childhood is spent in happiness. Then, as we got older the boredom of repetition takes over.

And now, as I learnt, I was alive again!

After 2 months of regular swimming, I could swim 3/4th of a length before I gave up and walked to the end. The regular swimmers acknowledged my presence and encouraged me. They told me they were impressed by my progress (I was too!) and that one day it would all happen. (How? How?) After 6 lengths, I felt spent. I was clearly out of shape. I felt as though I was battling the slog overs of a one-day cricket match. Between the 28th and 40th kilometres of a marathon! The most challenging game of mental strength and physical ability.

I had reached rock bottom. The only way I could go was up

June 2012.
6 months to SCMM 2013.

I spent the entire summer without running, under the guise of my learning to swim, awaiting the monsoon. Heat was my favourite enemy, including the usual tardiness of the mundane stuff. I was not a new marathon runner any more- so the dedication to continue training was just not there. When the monsoon finally arrived, rain was scarce. It was too late for me to look for any more excuses not to run, I just needed to get my act together and start! At the same time the previous year, it was one month after we had registered and committed to the event. I was in peak training mode, running half marathons regularly with ease.

This year, I almost registered for the half marathon as my hands trembled when I had to tick the box saying 42.195km. Just because I remembered running the SCMM 2012 did not mean that my body did too!

Running the marathon for the first time was a test to prove that I could do it physically. Running a marathon a second time is a mental game, for which I needed to forget the pain of the first and start afresh. This year I wanted to go for it all, to cross train extensively to support my running. I had learnt this from Santa, a 60-year-young fellow runner, who had moved into a whole new league with his dedication to running and cycling.

With four months left for SCMM January 2013, I thought I would make running a priority and work towards bettering my last year's time. Secretly, I wished I had not run my debut race as well as I had, as it was a difficult time to match with last-minute training. So here I began, running 4 days a week. Slowly, but as per plan.

But life takes its own course. Come week two and a crisis happened at work. Things spun out of control and each waking minute was consumed by work, thinking about work and in wondering how I would find the time to get things done.

The stress was overwhelming. It took over my life. Running disappeared from my life, as did everything else.

As I ruminated over this thought at 9.15am on the first Sunday of November, over a cup of coffee, after a traumatic 18km run, I realized that all through my run, thoughts about work had been racing through my mind. And then I saw the light: the confusion within us is really what we need to clear. Over the last month, my excuse for not running was work. The weakness of my mind conquered my discipline. I had told myself, this is a difficult time and I should let it pass, assuming that once it blew over things would normalize and I would go back to my running as per schedule. But I realised then, that by then, something else would emerge to challenge me.

To run well and to follow a routine is a simple task when all is running smoothly. It is a part of our life and we go with the flow day after day. But it is when life becomes a whirlwind that we need to rise above the mess and actually streamline and prioritize. In retrospect, I find it very hard to believe that I could not find even 4 hours a week to run in an entire month. The fact is that I would have worked better had I been running because my mind would have been clear.

My laziness had cost me. I used to breeze through 25km and last year at this time, in November, I was pushing 32km. I had run the 18km badly as I was carrying the baggage of a whole month!

All I needed was a good run to feel lighter.
I had learned at last that work is a means of sustenance, but running is food for soul!
Discipline and motivation were the two factors I would now need to keep within my sights, and blank out all the rest.

Oh, what a struggle the training season was. I had lost my rhythm, my stamina, and discovered that my legs had a mind of their own. Since the 2012 marathon my legs had smartened up. They had learned to stand up for themselves. They refused to do my bidding anymore. They had found a way to assert themselves, no matter how much I tried to control them.
The constant bickering between my brain and my legs resonated with the altercations between a rebellious teenager and their hapless mother.

Me vs My Muscles: M vs M. Part I

Me: C'mon you guys. Wake up and move! Savio has said we are doing 8 X 800s today!

Muscles: Are you crazy? Haven't you had enough?

Me: You've had a long break. Now c'mon, you've rested a long time. I have been kind to you.

Muscles: Dude! Have you forgotten how you completely and fully abused us?

Me: Oho, chalo now, be good, and remember how much fun it used to be. And it's not so hard once you get used to it.

Muscles (getting angry now): Are you even listening? You don't seem to be getting it! You keep pushing us again and again, and when we do listen to you, and do as you say, you simply push us harder and harder. (In a softer voice) You never listen to us...

Me (trying to pacify them): This time it will be different. We will ease into it and you won't even realize when it becomes harder...

Muscles: That's what you ALWAYS say!

Me: Ok guys. Stop whining. It's time for action!

Muscles (mumble): Whatever. We might as well do it, there is no point in arguing with her. She does whatever she wants to anyway!

SCMM 2013.
The second marathon.

The three of us started together. I ran the first half at a regular long run pace, and planned to step it up in the last 5-6km. But it took a lot of determination to pick up my tired legs and push myself mentally. It consumed my entire being to keep going. But I stuck at it, with only one single thought, that I should keep going, and that this too, shall end.

4:33 hours.

Thank god I took less time than last year!

There is a lot of repetitive activity in running and one needs to learn how to handle it. You need to find the techniques with which you can train the mind as well as your body. You need to maintain the same level of concentration when you're in a race as when you're training. It is no use imagining you will miraculously develop that focus on race day. There are things you may not be able to do now, but with a positive frame of mind, anything is possible. Remaining positive is one of the most precious qualities in an athlete. That, and the ability to stay focussed and disciplined.

The success of a sportsman rests on his (or her) capacity to suffer, even to enjoy suffering. You learn to accept that if you have to run 21km, you have to run, whether you do it in 2 hours 15 minutes or 2 hours 45 minutes. You just do it. It demonstrates endurance.

Endurance is an important word for marathoners. It expresses a Spartan philosophy of life that is uncommon today, where the principle of pleasure reigns supreme. On days when the body rebels and the pain seems too much, you've got two roads: tell yourself you've had enough and leave or be prepared to suffer and keep going.

The choice is between enduring and giving up. This is what separates the champions from the mere runners.

After all, it's the things you achieve with great effort that you value most.
The greater the effort, the greater the value.
Just grin and bear it.
Because he who conquers wins.

Shake off the lethargy
With the pain of the last race behind me.
No white sugar, no white bread,
Yes, dry fruits and protein shakes.
One banana and 5 dates,
a strong runner makes.
Stretch and foam roll,
Work towards the new goal.
Up the mileage, up the pace,
Get the Garmin ready to race!
Time to shift gear,
SCMM 2014 I am here.

6

GOAL AND STRATEGY

Immediately after completing both my previous marathons (SCMM 2012 and 2013), I felt that I wasn't broken. That seems a little ridiculous considering I had just run 42.2km, but I really wasn't spent. Instead, I thought that I could have gone on for a couple of kilometres more! As I checked my certificates, I discovered that I had cruised at a constant conversation pace throughout my runs. The realisation dawned that I hadn't push hard enough. Yes, I ran the distance. I did well. I struggled a bit in the last few kilometres, but it wasn't heart-wrenching. I had grown up believing that participation was important, not winning. But I found myself wondering...was it about timing? Was it also about doing well?

The truth was that I could have done better. This was not my best.

Maybe taking it easy was part of my personality. I just did the bare minimum required to do reasonably well. There was no use in persecuting yourself in trying to excel, when above average was enough. Maybe it was the hardships that I had faced in life that made me conserve my strength instead of expending it all. To play it safe in case of a crisis. This had become second nature to me as I held the family together. But now that we had all found our own grooves, I could break out and take risks. We had security and stability, and were more comfortable in our skins than ever.

I was ready to test the waters, or more literally, to test how fast I could run. I had to allow myself to go. I needed to give it all I had, so that I felt spent. I needed to feel the satisfaction of knowing I had pushed myself to the limit, at least, if not beyond.

I needed liberation. I had to break the barriers. Expose myself to uncertainty. I had to train my mind to give it all. To see if I could get it all.

I needed to construct an armour-plated mind.

Me vs. my Mind (M vs. M: Part II)

Savio's command was 8 x 800s at Priyadarshini Park.
Mind: Oh no! Two full rounds of PDP, non-stop with jogging rest. All 800s under 4 minutes. How? How? It will never happen!
Me (aloud): I hate 800s! Why? Why?
Savio (growls): Because they're good for you!
Me: I can't do it.
Mind (with a straight face): Yeah, you're not strong enough to do it...
Me: I agree, but may as well start, since I have to finish it. (Taking a deep breath) Ok, here goes.
Lap 1 time: 3.58 minutes
Mind: You've managed the first one, not bad! (Smirking) Let's see you do the rest...

Me: I will just keep going, I don't have a choice!

After completing 5 more laps, all barely under 4 minutes...averaging 3.58/3.57 minutes...
Me: I've done well! And I can easily do 2 more. Yes I'm tired, but I really want to kill it now!
Mind (thinking, with a grim look): Oh no! That sounds dangerous.
Me: You see now, how I fly! My fastest 800m is all set to happen.

After doing the 7th 800 in 3.45 minutes...
Me: See! I told you...I have done it!
Mind (in a small voice): Yes, you have.
Me: And now, the workout ends anyway, so I may as well go my fastest and give it my best.
Mind (thinking): Wow, what spirit
Me (after the 8th 800m): Hahahahaha! What a great workout...I just flew today!
Mind (grudgingly): Yes, it does feel good.
Me: Beat you again!
Mind (in an ever smaller voice): As always.
Me: But then how come you always get the better of me when I begin?
Mind: Because it is easy to create a doubt in your head when you believe that the task you have set out to accomplish is difficult and unachievable.
Me: But how do I know I can do it unless I actually do it?
Mind: Hahahaha! You don't! So there is always a crack within which I can plant the seed of uncertainty. Then you feed it on your own.
Me: Oh!
Mind: I don't do anything. Depending on your insecurities, that seed either grows, or you squash it. Usually, (in a smug voice), you

feed it well, and it grows, grows to incredible proportion, and most times without reason.

For a change I am speechless.

Mind (continuing): You do this to yourself as you don't have any faith in yourself and your capabilities. I am here to help you, to support you. But if you can't take my help, what can I do?

I am stunned.

Mind: You allow the whispers to find a home in your head. They settle down in dark corners in such a way that you don't even realize that they exist. Then these ghosts strike, sometimes with reason, but most times without reason.

Me (accusingly): And you enjoy this game?

Mind (smiling): Why not? You invite the devil into your head and allow it to exorcise you! I'm only watching the duel.

Me: What the hell!

Mind (gently): Then deal with it.

Me (feebly, tired, defeated): Yes, I should.

Mind: Don't be so dejected! We are on the same side, remember?

Me (brightening): Yes, that's true.

Mind: So come on then! Take the next challenge head on and see the result. Train your mind, the way you train your body.

Me: You mean you'll actually listen to me?

Mind: I usually don't listen to anyone, but if you don't tell anybody, then I will share a secret with you. Who doesn't want to be on the side of a winner?

Me: I agree. Everyone loves a success story!

Mind: So when you really want it, you will make me an ally, and use my strength. I will be by your side, and see you through your dark times, the most trying times. We will rise to the occasion together!

2013 was a big year for me, as my son, Arnav was going to sit his tenth standard board exams in March 2014. His Prelim exams and my marathon would be around the same time in January 2014. Just as I wanted to train harder and run faster than I had ever done, I motivated him too. He needed to do better than his best to get the required marks for admission in a good junior college, and I wanted to complete the 2014 marathon in 4 hours 20 minutes.

To complete the marathon in 4 hours and 20 minutes, I had to run each km in just over 6 minutes. Mathematically, it was 6 minutes/km to finish in 4:12 hours, and add a few minutes for the uphill, fatigue and weaving through the crowd. Since most of us run a couple of hundred metres more than the stipulated 42.2km due to the turns on the road and the weaving, 4:20 hours would be my dream finish. I ran my last half marathon in Hyderabad earlier in the year in 2:08 hours at the 6 minutes/km pace. It seemed audacious that I was attempting to run the entire distance of the marathon at this pace.

Yes, I was going out on a limb here by setting a target. But I did not want to settle with whatever time I could manage during the race.

I had decided I would work towards the time I desired.

Life was a pendulum swinging between his books and my running.

Arnav would have to now get a grip (I had been saying this for almost 3 terms now) and tighten his belt.

In order for me to better my eventual result I needed to change my training. Intensify it. I could not continue doing what I had been doing for the past two years and expect a dramatic change. I had to do things I had not done thus far.

I was a veteran of comebacks. I knew I could do whatever it was I set my mind to do. With experience, will and dedication I was ready for another paradigm shift.

The strategy had been drawn out:
1. Speed training.
2. Hill workout.
3. Endurance.
4. Yoga/ Stretching.

Of all of these, I felt endurance was the easiest. Give me a long run, any distance at an easy pace and I am game for it. But make me run at a pace, even a short distance and I get stressed. And hills! Those were another challenge. I had identified my strengths and weaknesses. This was what I needed to work on. My fears. And hone my skills.

Establish.
Strategize.
Practice.
Execute.
Review.
E.S.P.E.R.

Tempo runs were at the race course: continuous 2km loops, several of them, at half marathon pace in alternating directions. The soft mud track made the workout harder. The running in loops made the brain work more. And the pace, aaaah the pace. That was always the hardest, but I learnt to run without talking, only looking inward, only focussing on the result.

April 2013, Sunday long run
An awakening

I ran with Mulraj and Rakesh. Both experienced runners, who are a notch above me. I started with the thought that I only needed to keep up with them till halfway. The plan was to then fade away as they would run further and complete their 15km, which was a bit too much for me. So I planned to simply ditch them at the 6km mark and turn around and run back at my slow easy pace (This was a complete deviation from the training plan that I ought to be following!).

With friendly banter we reached the 6km mark. As I said good bye, they surprised me and said that they would return with me! There went my escape plan.

Along the next couple of slow easy kilometres , they discussed various strategies on how to pick up pace for the last 4km, Fartlek (a combination of fast running and easy running for every kilometre) or Indian file, where one person leads for a kilometre, fast, and then the next one takes over, running even faster)? My heart just sank! The trial had begun.

My head was trying to work out the most feasible way to evade this trauma. I had found my defence: "I am a frail woman"! I said. This was shot down in one second by Rakesh who said, "Hence, we as men, need to escort you till the very end!" DOOM!

I was leading the first leg of the Indian file from the beginning of Marine Drive (3.5km left from where we were) and was out of breath by the end of my kilometre at the signal. I slowed to a walk and told them to carry on. But no!

Past the flyover, Rakesh lead the pack. Huffing and puffing, I managed to keep up until the last 20m, when I gave up. They slowed down as well, allowing me to catch my breath. Then Mulraj shifted the gear into cruise control for the last kilometre. Oh my! I felt my lungs would burst as I followed Rakesh's advice to lengthen my stride, and Mulraj's to move my arms vigorously!

What a finish! I had an out of body experience!

The pace was unnatural and my mental state was surreal. I was in a new place. An unfamiliar place. I had to visit this place often and make it my own. This was where I needed to be. A place which was bang on my path to a new training plan.

Our post-run breakfast was in honour of the five swimmers – Zarir, Byram, Rupali, Vidhi and Rajesh -- who had swum 100 lengths at CCI. Each of them swam as well as they ran, or maybe even better! They swam 2.3km in under an hour. That was a place where I wanted to be. A group I aspired to join.

Rakesh and Mulraj are runners I aspired to keep up with. Motivation, hard work and discomfort would get me there.

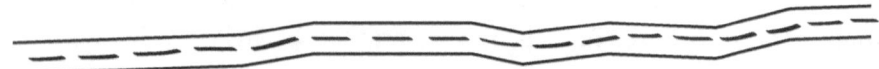

All these years I have been a steady runner who struggles a bit in the last 10km. This year, 2014, I was determined to run strong till the end. So I introduced a new element in my long runs (apart from the usual intervals and tempo runs) called the fast finish. This meant was that I would run at an easy pace for most of my long run, but would speed up to marathon pace or even faster for the last few kilometres. This was a huge test for my mind. I, who had always been an easy runner, had to now push myself.

I had to focus.
Develop concentration.
Maintain my form.

As per this plan the first thing I had to do was to find my race pace. So I strapped on my long lost Garmin (a watch for sports people which can record distance, pace, route and other data) and started monitoring my runs. Each and every one of them. Distance as well as pace. The total mileage of the week was most important. Savio would always say, if you have to run 40km in one day then in a week you should do a minimum of 60-70km. These numbers scared me, but once I made my Excel sheet, it was a matter of planning the runs over 4 days a week.

On advice of my friend and fellow marathoner Sandeep, I added

Saturday as a fifth running day. Only 10-12km to get my legs "tired" for the long run on Sunday. This principle would simulate the last 10km of a marathon, which he said, was the key to the finish time of the marathon. We routinely train for 32km, what happens beyond that is anybody's guess. Train for that, he said.

As a result, I was running Fridays, Saturdays and Sundays consecutively. 50km over 3 days.

That was more than a marathon distance each weekend! Of which the last few kilometres were at race pace, on tired, almost dead legs!

This punishing schedule did one thing for sure: it killed my social life. I was living in a perpetual state of exhaustion. Life was a blur. Days were passing from run to run, with work, studying and the rest filling up the time in between. This was not an easy way to live. Each time I felt myself cracking, and weakness entering my mind, I would look at my beautifully colour-coded log sheet and cringe at the red cells (workouts not done) and orange cells (incomplete workouts). They were few and far between, but even then, they would glare at me like an infuriated mother who would throw her arms up in despair while chastising her wayward teenager. With a sullen face, I would cancel my plans and turn my alarm on for the next day.

Training like this was therapeutic. There was no thinking. It was only action. The brain had to remain focussed on the goal of that particular workout. No wavering. No doubts. This toughened my mind and spirit. It helped me to fill in the small cracks of my heart, to obliterate all remnants of pain, and heal myself completely. Just when you think that you don't have anything more to give, you look deep within and discover something hidden in the dark unexplored crevices. I was in a new place, mentally and physically, in life and in running.

When we train at this intensity we need to look after our muscles, as quick recovery and injury prevention is paramount. Post the Sunday long run, I spent my evenings watching TV with my legs soaked in salted hot water. On weekdays, TV accompanied my stretching and foam rolling. I had never watched so much TV in 4 months ever before!

Friends, the West Wing, the Big Bang Theory, MasterChef...I had hated watching TV over the last few years. Earlier, it emphasised my loneliness and then I thought it was a waste of time. Suddenly I had found new use for the idiot box!

From previous experiences of running the SCMM route, I realised that my Achilles' Heel was Peddar Road. The thought of running up the road paralysed me. To face this fear head on, I did several repeats of the uphill section at a furious pace. I did all I could and hoped that this training would bear fruit on race day.

Early in November, I did my first Fast Finish, clocking 6.10 minutes per km for the last 6km. Not bad, I thought. But I felt I could have given more. So in 2 weeks, when it was time for my next test, I attempted the last 10km at the pace of 6 minutes/km, and managed that beautifully as well! What was going on? I was pushing myself harder and harder and the boundaries were extending with ease. Being pleasantly surprised with myself, I decided to get ambitious and go all out for the next Fast Finish. 13km at 5.50 minutes/km.

That was done too. I was on a roll. I was not used to this. Week after week I was being pushed farther and farther out of my comfort zone. In a new place, maybe the magic happened here!

This engaged my mind and completing the run at the target pace gave me a huge sense of accomplishment. Much to my dismay, no conversation was possible at this pace!

As I increased the Fast Finish pace each fortnight, the pace of my tempos and intervals increased too. It took more courage to start the harder workouts as they looked more threatening at the start than the benign easy pace runs. I would dread every speed workout. I would get anxious about it, and successfully convince myself that it was going to be very hard, and that I would not manage. With a sense of trepidation and a deep breath, I would begin the workout and then just go with the flow. It wasn't easy. Especially the middle laps. In an 8-lap workout, the 5th and 6th laps were always the most difficult. Come lap 7, I could see the end and it became a breeze. This mind game taught me fortitude. Despite the mental fatigue, I had to go on. I should simply accept what I had to do. Then, once the ball was rolling it would only stop once I made it stop. I was clocking speeds which were alien to me, and much to my shock I was able to sustain them over the required distances. Mile repeats, 2km repeats at the racecourse, 8km loops. All these were under 5.30 pace.

How did that happen? My Garmin had never seen any sustained pace beginning with the number "5". I was a "6" runner! I just could not fathom how I was able to do this. My body was working in harmony with my mind. Each and every nerve and fibre was working in unison to propel me towards the target pace. I had become a "serious" runner! I ran with single-mindedness, grit and core strength. Something had changed within me. I was on track for my goal of my personal best at SCMM 2014.

At the end of each workout my brain was frazzled, but the sweet juice of happiness enveloped the folds of my brain as I reflected upon what I had just done!
Each lap.
Each run.
Every day.
This was my bank from which I would draw courage.

The third week of December posed a real challenge for me.
The week of my maximum mileage.
The week of a close family wedding.

Maithili, my niece, who is very dear to me, was getting married. I was conflicted. I wanted to enjoy the wedding, but did not want my training to suffer. Since the wedding functions started on a Friday evening and went on for a few days, I decided I would complete my weekly schedule by Friday morning. That was the only time that my running schedule was modified for my social life. At all other times, it was the other way.

Friday morning. My first and last 32km run of the season. My last Fast Finish. I was running with Rahul, who would run at his pace. My run was the first 16km at easy pace, and the second 16km at 5.45 min/km.

Mentally, I was afraid.

Physically, I was unsure.

So I called upon Abbas. He is a gold polisher by day and one of the fastest runners of the group. His special quality, however, is that he has an in-built Garmin. He can run at any pace with ease. Once I told him my plan he told me not to worry and that he would make sure that it was bang on target.

Oh what a run it was! After the first slow 16km, I was raring to go for my critical second half. He picked up the pace gradually and held it. We ran strong. Steady. Unwavering. We even sprinted that last 500m and pushed the final pace of the second lap to 5.43 min/km. What a finish. I was elated! A seemingly painless and effortless run but a hard, rewarding one.

As I tested my capabilities, I found that I was capable of a lot more, of giving a lot more. I was awakened. My mind was charged. I could now see a plethora of possibilities in my range which I never thought I could even dream of! This year my training of all these years would bear fruit.

And then it happened. I started to dream big.

Could I run the marathon at 5:45 pace instead of the original target of 6? Could I actually shave 15 seconds/km for the entire 42.2km? Yes, I had never run even a half marathon at the 5:45 pace, but all was going well and I told myself I can run the marathon at 5:45. I will make it happen. Fuelled with all this positivity and confidence, I grew as a person, letting go of self doubt, with my faith and belief increasing. I was a living example of preparedness being a sure shot sign of success.

With the training done and dusted, only the taper remained. This is what we call the relatively easier 3 weeks of training just before the race, when we run shorter distances, at slightly slower paces, just to stay in touch with the sport, and to rest our legs, allowing them to recover in time for the race. I was free to enjoy the wedding and all the other parties.

Any type of training which pushes our mind and body is hard. But once it is over, we can relax and enjoy the fruits of our labour. Marathon training takes a big toll, physically as well as mentally. I had a blast at the wedding, as I switched off my brain, and made polite conversation with all and laughed with the family. They came from far and wide. They had seen me over the years. Been with me and helped me through my ups and downs. As my well-wishers, they were genuinely happy to see what a long way I had come, and how well we were all doing.

Along with that, though, I got a fair share of "concerned relatives" enquiring about my health, as I looked so thin, so tired, so washed out! I took all these as compliments and tucked in to all the delicious wedding goodies to my heart's content. I was on holiday. This was my weekend off after 4 long months of discipline, rules and hard work. And maybe that's why I enjoyed the wedding so much! The timing was perfect.

Arnav's studying was done. All that remained were the exams. I had done the best I could. Nagging him. Feeding him. Helping him. Now both of us had to hope that the finals would go without a hitch. We had both prepared to the best of our abilities.

5 years ago I never thought that "marathoner" would be a word used to describe me. It is funny how my identity has been redefined, or should I say created. After my first name, the first thing that people learn about me is that I run marathons.

Gasp!

All my other labels have faded in comparison. And the conversation takes a turn towards my passion.

Yes, I run a lot.

No, not everyday, only four-five times a week.

Hmmm, how much? Almost 60-70km a week during the peak training period.

No, I don't run 42km regularly! (Huh?)

Yes, it tires me.

Of course it's hard.

No, I don't get paid.

And no, I don't win. I NEVER win.

7

FEAR AND READINESS

SCMM 2014: 21km:
Half way mark

By kilometre 21, we are a quartet with Raghu, a runner from Bangalore who also was a 4 hours 30 minutes full marathon runner. But today he is running for his personal best! He has been tailing us the whole way and after 2 hours we officially induct him into our bus. More conversation! Whew!

We cross the mid-point of the race. I reflect upon how far I have come in my life...literally and figuratively! From a non-runner to a marathoner, and now a writer in lieu of the runs. Along this journey, I have overcome numerous hurdles and broken several barriers.

My life until 2003 was sheltered and cushy. I only did what I wanted to, by choice, be it work or pleasure. Most of my life, I read world news and literature. I abhorred the pink pages and anything finance related. Accounting was akin to Greek and Latin for me. Actually, I am willing to learn Greek, but can't say the same about accounting.

Numbers. Balance sheets. Money matters. Car repairs. All of it was too difficult for me.

Similarly, I had developed several notions about running over the years. Can't run in the sun! Can't run on Friday! Can't run at Race Course! Can't run long! Can't run without music!
Slowly and steadily over the last decade, all my cant's have become became cans. As I opened my mind towards them, the doors appeared.

Now I read the Economic Times and the Mint. I listen to the budget speech. Discuss tax laws. Know the interest rates. I understand what these numbers really mean.

When we focus on what we are willing to change, it becomes a mountain range: a long hard road, but a road we can follow nonetheless.

As a part of the training for heat, I actually timed my runs to complete them in the heat. I even started a run at 9 am on a Sunday.

I did all my tempo runs on Fridays at the race course. I started early at 5.15 am, ran to the race course as a part of the warm up, ran in circles until I got dizzy, ran back to cool down and met the kids at the bus stop to send them off to school. All by 7.15am.

As for music, I now use it only during races, and that too in the second half. I gave it up a long time ago on advice of Neepa, an accomplished ultra-marathoner. I have known Neepa since I was a child, and I don't think either of us had imagined that we would be marathoners in our later years. Neepa and Amit are legendary in Indian running circles. They introduced the Comrades Marathon to us.

I met Neepa after several years at Amit's book launch in 2010. At that time, while signing the book, she wrote for me that she hoped to see me running beside her at the next marathon. I smiled and told her that I didn't have the mental fortitude and the physical strength to keep running for 42km. I thought I'd never be able to do it.

SCMM 2014: 22km.

The pack of Vishal, Rohan, Raghu and I stick together for the next 7-8km. We motivate each other and get into rhythm. Raghu however cannot keep up. As we reach Worli Seaface, the other two boys also feel the heat. They falter. Rohan is a young, fit boy, who plays squash at a competitive level. Over the last 3 years, he would show up for the marathon, train for only 2 months and on race day, and pip all of us! Not this year. This year, at kilometre 28, I leave them. For the first time I am ahead of them. I gather all my courage and decide to keep going. I have managed to maintain the required pace. I am not tired yet. I amaze myself!

In an endurance athlete's life, pain is never far away. Pain is little more than a conversation between body and your brain. That's another reason why a fit mind is so important.

The brain is constantly trying to impose limits on what it thinks it can achieve. We should constantly question it; fight it, which means enduring pain. Successful athletes relish their relationship with pain. Not the mechanical kind, which tells us when something has broken down, but emotional pain. Pain is our brain's way, like a caring parent, of telling us that it doesn't like how hard it's working right now! We need to challenge that.

So it's up to you to find the motivation to win. This is your only chance. Squeeze all your will into the race. The truth is that you can do it. What you can never allow is failure because of loss of will. You can feel like you have lost if you don't reach your target due to an unforeseen situation, but you can't admit defeat because you failed to give it your best shot. That is a crime.

So rise above the pain and exhaustion and summon up the desire to run, the desire to be a winner. Adrenaline and the mind will triumph over the pain. The defeatism will go and the need to win will prevail. The challenge of overcoming your predicament is not something to fear but to cherish. So hang in there and push yourself to the very limit of your abilities.

We all have a little voice inside all of us that urges us to fulfil our potential. Some of us can't hear it amidst the din, others are too afraid of it, to go for it and to fail. That fear, is immobilizing.

But then you realise that the fear doesn't exist.

This thought process doesn't develop overnight. It takes months and maybe years to put into practice. Hours of pounding the road, enduring the weather, injuries, mental breakdowns, and even with all this bouncing back. Coming back with a stronger resolve than ever before.

This resolve is easy to have in the calm before the storm. Resolve is a breeze when your commitment is not tested. But if you work diligently, then when the true test comes, this resolve will make you rise to the occasion. Over the last few weeks, I have developed one motto: that I will not stop. I will keep going, just putting one foot ahead of the other and go on and on.

SCMM 2014: 32km

I maintain the same steady rhythm and pace until the 35km mark. I am all alone; I have passed some good runners who have run out of wind. They are all strong runners, who run half marathons much faster than me. However, today does not seem to be their day! With me, now, my wily mind is playing new tricks on me by the minute. I dread the impending doom awaiting me at Peddar Road only a few hundred meters away. My relationship with hills is not very good. Actually, it is awful.

August 3rd 2012.
Wednesday "Hills!" with Savio, 6.00 am.

Another scheduled hill run. A sense of dread overcomes me. As much as I enjoy and look forward to my long Sunday runs, I hate the hill workout. This is a 12km route of rolling, almost mountainous slopes, where even cars need to be driven in first gear! This is the neighbourhood in which I spent my childhood. This is where my parents' house is, where I went to school and art class and where all my friends lived. Sweet memories reside in these treacherous inclines. They brought me no comfort that day.

I started my workout and my goal was only to run it non-stop, however slow that would be. The fact that an uphill, sooner or later, made way for the downhill, was a big motivating factor.
I ran with Rajesh, at a pace which was more like a fast walk. Rajesh is a steady runner. I have never seen him give up or speak in a defeatist tone. Once he sets his goal, he rests only once it is completed. He always runs with a heart rate monitor. For a little bit during the hill run, Yash was with us. His advice to Rajesh was to ditch the monitor because it plays with your mind! The mind is very fickle! Anything can scare it! This advice to Rajesh struck a chord with me.

Our mind determines our actions. The more we fear failure, the greater the chances of failure. I realise my mistake. The repetitive statements about my intense dislike of hills have actually fuelled my negativity.

They reiterate my fear. They haunt me when I run. They

make each step harder.

I need to tackle this head on. As Rajesh said at the beginning of the run, my mantra has to be "I love hills". Now I understand why I need to make the enemy my ally.
I need to change my beliefs regarding pain and fatigue. I view these feelings as feelings of failure. Instead, they are an opportunity to experience a breakthrough in my personal level of achievement. I am feeling pain and fatigue because I have pushed myself closer to the perceived limit of my ability. How great will it feel once I have pushed through these feelings and come out on the other side, now with limitless possibilities? I shift my mindset from the negative to the positive and all of a sudden, pain and fatigue are no longer enemies but friends. Friends running with you on your way to achieving your goal. Pain is weakness leaving my body.

I ran the hills. All 12km! I was steady in the first half, but I wanted to give up in the second half. The only thing motivating me to complete this run was the concession which Savio gave me. When he saw me huffing and puffing, he moved the stick with the carrot closer and said that I could leave out the last slope. Relieved that my agony would end early, I went on. Upon reaching the last hill (the one that I could have left out) I went ahead and did that as well. I just could not bear the thought of giving up. I finished it. But I walked a lot. I gave up at many points instead of running and fighting it out.

Post the run, Savio had very encouraging words for me. After two weeks, he said, when you are stronger, you will be able to complete the entire 14km circuit with ease. I look forward to that.

Success is moving from failure to failure with enthusiasm.

All these years, I had let my fear control me. My fear was controlling my mind. Now my mind would control my body, as I would have the will to conquer the hills. I needed to empower myself. The first time I ever ran the hills – 3 years ago – I used to think "the hills are alive, and my legs are dead!" Next week, I hope to say, "Thank you, for the hills, and strength I found to climb them."

SCMM 2014: 35km.

It is an unbelievable feeling to run up the most difficult patch – 1.5km up Peddar Road at kilometre 35 – and smile at the end of it. To greet the waiting crowd, who have waited for me for at least a couple of hours, to hear them encourage me and to cheer me. They have been there for me, and to salute the spirit of all of us runners, year after year. Despite all my bravado, I still surrender to the steepest incline of Peddar Road, as I walk up 20m, and then I start a slow jog, just in time to save face. With an incredible sense of pride and community, I hide the pain of the last 9 minutes, of the last 10 years, hold my head up high and wave to the bystanders feeling like a star. I pass friends and family, all rooting for me. I increase my pace with their encouraging words and once the uphill distance is done with, I start to fly. As I approach my building, I am in high spirits because I know a large crowd is waiting for me. A fellow runner nicknamed me the "Celebrity of Peddar Road". The hard work is done and the hardest part of the race is over. Now there is only the last stretch – 6km to go. I blaze downhill, with

Rhea and Aadit (my niece and nephew) in tow, as I run my fastest kilometre of the entire race with them!

The last 6km, Sandeep told me once, is "Best Effort". When I asked him what he meant, he said that at that point in the race it is hard to predict the condition of the brain. By then, the body is completely exhausted, and all your energy reserves depleted. What happens henceforth is purely a mind game. This is the time to dig deep.

I had trained very hard this year. Pushed my body and mind to their utmost limits. During training I accomplished paces and distances which I never thought I was capable of. I was all set to continue at my target race pace. I just had to do it.

Suddenly the life rules I had learned from long ago come flooding back to me. Only when I was ready to change did I really change. That was the sliver of light which first entered through the door. That gave me hope and the courage to open the door fully and allow the light in.

This readiness is the biggest motivation for anything that we want to accomplish. Readiness implies a degree of concentration and eagerness. We do our best when we are physically, mentally and emotionally ready to learn, to apply and to push. We need to have a clear objective, a strong purpose and a definite reason to overcome all the difficulties which we are bound to encounter along the way.

The effort to keep at it, day after day as per schedule is paramount.

Every practice session makes us stronger as we move closer toward the goal. Once the effort is regular, we see the effect of this. This in turn has an emotional effect. It is a satisfying feeling to see progress. And this is directly proportional to motivation.

Each lesson need not be entirely successful. We don't need to master anything in the first shot. All lessons are small steps towards the ultimate goal. While making the effort we may encounter feelings of defeat, frustration and exhaustion. This only makes us stronger. They condition our brain and can be channelized in a positive way. It depends entirely on us to extract what we think we have gained from each session. This is the positivity which will get us through on race day. This is what lays the foundation for the last 10km, which is when the race really begins! When the mind gives up, we have to dig deep and bring out these strong, unshakeable positive memories. All this hard work will give us the confidence we require on D-day.

Along with my running, I have spent all of last year reading classics by John Milton. The recurrent theme in most of his early work is his anticipation of doing something big in his life. He wrote for 25 years: poetry, prose, sonnets, essays, waiting for the big idea to strike. And at age 59, he wrote the world's greatest epic poem, Paradise Lost.

I'm nowhere close to Milton in any way, but I see a parallel here. We all itch to do something big, but we embark on that road only when we are ready. Ready to commit. When the time comes and the stars align.

These are all words of the old and the wise. All making sense to me now. Now that I have matured enough to understand them. They have now become a reality of my life.

And thus I run to complete the best race of my life, till date.

SCMM 2014: 38km

At Chowpatty, Samir runs an inspiring 200m with me. He restores my confidence for a great finish at a consistent pace. I look strong and feel strong.
The battle between my mind and my fatigued legs has started to get ugly! After every kilometre I push the pace up for 20-30 steps and then go steady. It is a glorious feeling to pass by the brave marathoners who have now slowed down to a walk. Each step reinforces my belief. I am going to make it happen.

Failure is not an option.
I have not come here to walk!

With these thoughts, I forge ahead. My strength is the bank of good wishes from all the people who were kind enough to pass positivity to me via their text messages, phone calls and blessings. I pass by more family at Marine Drive and Churchgate. By now, I have run out of steam and greet them only with a tiny wave of my left hand. I have only one focus.

With 500m to go, my partners from my previous marathons, Raina (my good luck charm) and Sukhpreet pace me. I struggle to keep up with them.

I see the 300m mark approach.
Then the finish line.
An open road ahead of me.
Everything blurs except for the digital clock, mounted high on top of the finish line, I leave everyone and everything as I sprint past the 100 year old neoclassical buildings, past the cheering multitudes towards the iconic VT station.

SCMM 2014: 4:09:21: My Personal Best.

23 minutes faster than my previous record. 11 minutes faster than my target time, with an average pace of 5 minutes 50 seconds per kilometre! I have done it. I am a winner!
I am in tears at the finish. My tears not of joy or sadness, but just relief. Relief that it is over. Tears of accomplishment, fatigue, and that I can stop pushing, and finally relax.

I had set a target.
Trained for it.
Achieved it.

All the hard work paid off.

All my words worked. Words and dreams, which are strong enough to start wars. My victory is a combination of the wishes from each person who thought of me and prayed for me. They have contributed to the realisation of this dream.

It is now 4.25 am on Monday morning. I have been awake since 3 am because of the excruciating pain in my back and legs. I feel that they are made of wood and they will crack and fall off at any minute! But it has all been worth it.
In one month all this pain will be forgotten, as I set new targets, and gear up to push myself harder than ever before.

The end of something is merely the beginning of something else.

New horizons await.
A new frontier beckons.

Life has come full circle.

Sanjana has turned 13. She is a budding ballerina and actress. She has found her passions and is walking the tight rope between extra-curricular activities and academics with ease. A fount of wisdom, she has grown to be a sensitive young girl, who will find her place in the world.
Arnav, 16, took his board exams in March 2014. As a result of his dedication, he scored great marks and today, is in the college of his choice. He is on the brink of independence. The motto of the college is "To provoke until they fly". I see that Arnav has already sprouted wings. He is itching to flap them wide and soar.

The last bit of the umbilical cord needs to be cut for him to stand by himself.

In a race or a sport, you practice. Practice what you have to do, until it becomes automatic. It becomes your default setting. Similarly in stressful social situations, when you don't have time to make a decision, time to think, the answer will come on its own. The one which is in the default setting. The one that you have spent an entire childhood practicing. Making the correct choice.

As I set my children free, I do hope that they believe these are my realities.

Trying to maintain good default settings of my own.

Trying to build love and respect. Trying to build endurance that will carry us when we have a load to carry.

Trying all these things – however imperfectly – messing up, dusting off and starting again.

Ketu would have been 45. I see our little girl and boy have turned into a pretty young lady and a handsome six-footer! He would have been proud of them.

He would have been wrapped around Sanjana's little finger and would have danced to the tune of Arnav's bass guitar.

I am nostalgic but not sad and there is a difference.
Time is flying, going by too fast. Perhaps faster than I thought.

> *"Long is the way, and hard, that out of hell leads up to light."*
> *John Milton, Paradise Lost, Book 2.*

The Route For The Race Of My Life:
SCMM 2014- MARATHON 42.195km

07:45AM
MIDWAY POINT 21km

MAHIM

SEA LINK

FULL CROWD SUPPORT

SHIVAJI PARK

28km

14km

THE NEVER-ENDING MIDDLE KILOMETERS: THE HARDEST

HAJI ALI

32km
ATRIA NSCI

9km

RACE COURSE

PERILOUS PEDDAR

35km
CELEBRITY OF PEDDAR

MUSCLE VS MIND

HALLELUJAH MOMENT SCMM 2011

5km

38km

SUN BEATING DOWN

CHOWPATTY

MARINE DRIVE

3km

04:09:21
FINISH

START/ FINISH LOCATION:C.S.T.
START TIME: 5:40am

2km
NARIMAN POINT

EPILOGUE

Why do we run marathons?

It's a question I've asked myself often.

There comes a point in every marathon, usually around kilometre 30 when I start to ask myself why I'm here, doing this to myself. At kilometre 36, I start promising myself that I'll never do this again. It is hard work, it is not fun, why would anyone do this to themselves, and no way, not ever again, will I do another one of these.

So far I've run 3 marathons, and 14 half marathons. Are all of us who run these long races gluttons for punishment? Or are we just plain crazy? People who don't run, or have never run the 42.2k monster don't get it. Before I ran one myself, it wasn't so much that I didn't get it, but it was more that I didn't think I would ever be able to run that far. I didn't think I was physically strong enough. At the time, I didn't understand that physically, it's simply a matter of training and building up to a certain endurance level.

But I also know that it's much, much more than that. In fact, I would say that running a marathon is actually more mental than physical. For me personally, it's about 99% mental. It takes a certain type of person to run marathons. We are obsessed people, who read everything we can about running and improving, and we're tough. We do what it takes, and not crossing the finish line is never an option.

Karen Armstrong, a historian, has the following theory. The mythology of the hero most probably began in the Palaeolithic age, and was part of the human subconscious from time immemorial. Rama, Arjuna, Hercules. Achilles, all seemingly ordinary people put into extraordinary situations. All cultures have developed similar mythologies about the heroic quest. The hero feels that there is something missing in his own life. So he leaves home and endures tough conditions and finds death-defying adventures. He fights monsters, climbs inaccessible mountains, traverses dark forests and, in the process, his old self dies, he gains new insight or skill, which he brings back to his people. The man becomes a hero as he rises to the occasion.

When people told these stories about the heroes of their lands, they were not simply hoping to entertain their listeners. These myths tell us what we have to do if we want to become better than we are. Every single one of us has to be a hero at some time in our lives.

There are parallels between a hero's journey and running a marathon. You cannot be a hero unless you are prepared to give up everything; there is no ascent to the heights without a prior descent into darkness, no new life without some form of death. Throughout our lives, we all find ourselves in situations in which we come face-to-face with the unknown, and it is the myth of the hero that shows us how we should behave.

This is where the entire idea of running a marathon as a hero's journey comes together for me. Even when we train for 4 months and do a couple of 30km runs, we don't really know what lies ahead when we stand at the start line of our first marathon. We're embarking on a road we've never travelled before. For most runners, going beyond your previous longest distance is uncharted territory, your very own personal struggle upwards from the ninth circle of hell. Even if you're running your fifth marathon, something happens to your body and mind around the 32km mark that pushes you into a place you don't often visit.

But when you persevere, when you go beyond the parameters of your old expectations and abilities, when you cross that finish line, your old self truly dies. The person who wears the medal at the finish line is not the same person who stood nervously at the start line.

Sure, afterwards, life goes on, you go back to work in a few days, but you've changed. You've learned something about yourself that can only be experienced by going farther than you've ever gone before.

This journey is nothing less than the adventure of the hero. The adventure of being alive. It's a journey of your own making, and the only person you can trust to reach the end is yourself. You have to trust that everything you've taught yourself up to that point is going to work, and that everything you rely on will do its job successfully: your legs, your mind, your strength, your endurance, your focus, your spirit, and your belief in yourself.

When it all comes together, when you finish the race, no matter what metaphorical monsters, inaccessible mountains, or dark forests you had to travel through, or all the years of being non-athletic, alcoholic, obese, unmotivated, lazy, or whatever shadow chases you, no matter how long it took you to get there, you become a hero to yourself.

You are the hero of your own story.

TIPS FOR NEW RUNNERS

Odds and ends from my running experience of 7000kms and 10 years (I would have reached the North Pole or London had I run this distance in a straight line!):

GEAR:

1.   *Clothes:* I have always run in tropical weather. Dri-fit tops and bottoms from most top brands are comparable. Only when you try a few will you know what suits you the best. I began running with regular track pants and Dri-fit t-shirts. Slowly the length of my pants reduced to three-fourth length. As my ankles became free and ventilated, I felt better. And then after joining the group, I gathered courage and started wearing shorter tights. More breathability for my lower body! Once I was able to ditch modesty, my uniform became a Nike racer back vest with Nike tempo shorts. The tank top allows free range of movement and reduces chafing in the underarm area. The shorts come with a tiny pocket for keys and gels, as well as built-in underwear. They are well aerated and

comfortable. By now, people are accustomed to seeing me leave the building, at wee hours of the morning in my strange attire, with strangers who are dressed as weirdly as me!

My friend Ashish used to run in track pants for the longest time, until one day he decided to jump into my shorts brigade. From that day on, he has only run in shorts. So for men, I would recommend shorts, the athletic kind (most have in-built underwear to prevent chafing) or bicycle tights. Cotton t-shirts for and long runs are a no-no. They cause severe chafing.

Do invest in good running attire. Once you have some sitting in your wardrobe it will ensure your regularity, especially when you think of the small fortune that you have spent on it!

Application of Vaseline: For longer runs do remember to lubricate all the areas of the body which are subjected to maximum friction: the inner thighs, chest area, under the sports bra for women, and on the nipples for men, under the arms and between the toes. There are some anti-chafing gels and creams available too. Vaseline has worked well for me.

2.   *Shoes:* This is a big worry for most of us. How I wish our shoes could make us better runners! But yes, runners research shoes on the internet, talk to other runners and many theories affect their decision on which is the right shoe for them. Your shoe will depend on many factors: your body type, your pronation, the surface you run on. Lighter runners can get away with lighter, minimal shoes. Others may need the more cushioned models. Brand loyalty is very high with shoes. Runners swear by their shoes once they are

comfortable in them. I began with Nike Shox 10 years ago. Went through 3 pairs. Then came Nike Zoom Vomeros. I think I used 5 pairs of those. And now, I have moved to a more minimal shoe, Brooks Pure Cadence. It is lighter than both my previous models, and feels more grounded, as it has minimal cushioning. I wore out 2 pairs last year, and have bought 2 new pairs this year. I alternate my shoes for each run. Because of the heavy mileage I put in, I need 2 pairs of shoes per year. For new runners, and those doing the half marathon, averaging 30-odd km per week, their shoes should last them a year. The average life of a shoe is 800-900km. I used to buy new shoes after every SCMM race, in February. The thing about these shoes is that they never look worn out. They only get beaten down from the midsole, which provides cushioning and stability. They feel "dead" when you run in them. Continued use will result in small niggles, shin splints or muscle fatigue. One disclaimer here: If you are happy with your shoes, my suggestion would be to stick with it. Why change something which is working for you?

Oh, the Laces: Unless you want the few minutes of illicit rest in the middle of a workout (I used to relish those moments) when the laces come off, do learn the correct way to tie them. There is a science to this little act- you need to double knot them. That means make another bow with the two ends of the bow (there are YouTube videos online showing you how) and they will NEVER open.

Do cut your toe nails to prevent them from banging against your shoes. A lot of runners get black toe nails from not doing this. When buying a pair of shoes do ensure you have half an inch of space in the front of your toes, as you feet will expand while running. Your toes also need to have enough room for motion, so ensure that you can wiggle them comfortably in the front of the shoe. This usually means that you need to buy shoes which are half-a-size bigger than your normal size.

3.   *Socks:* Socks, like shoes have a life too. So do use new socks every season, and maybe keep the old ones for casual use. In my laziness, I suffered a few years ago. The pain I got in my calves was inexplicable until I ditched my 2-year-old socks (in the middle of a training season) which still looked as good as new! Socks can be ultra light or cushioned, made of Dri-fit breathable material. I use the thin ones for speed work and keep the cushioned ones for longer runs.   There are also double-layered socks which prevent blisters. However for a half marathon or any shorter runs, most good quality cotton socks would work. I have been faithful to Nike over the years. I have seen some runners run in compression socks. These they say, keep the calves warm. Frankly, I think they look quite ridiculous and have never tried them.

4.   *Music:* A lot of long distance runners prefer to run without music, including me. When I began, however, my permanent partner was my iPod shuffle. It helped me take my mind off running, and made it seem easier. With time, as I became a better runner I was able to give it up. So if you are a beginner, and feel the need for music, then I would say run with it. As the running feels easier you can wean yourself off it. An iPod shuffle works the best by virtue of its size.

5.   *Timing gadget:* For example, a Garmin watch or any device which measures your speed and distance. When I started running, I just ran. I had a vague idea of the distance of various landmarks from my house. So based on that, I ran easy. I never really cared

about my speed. It remained fluid until I started running with Savio's Stars. That is when I understood the difference in speed and pace, and what it meant to do speed work. To run for fun is a great way to begin running. Once you are fitter, get a device with a simple stop watch if you are really keen to keep a log. Let your body dictate your pace. I bought a Garmin only when I registered for my first full marathon. Even after that, its primary use was to record the distance and time of our Sunday long runs.

TRAINING:

1.   *Regularity:* This is the most important part of learning anything new. We all know that practice makes perfect. Similarly, consistency makes you a better runner. Running takes time. It takes months of training to prepare for races and to build endurance. Dedication is the key. NO SHORTCUTS! If you are unable to run on the running day, do run a day before or after, or even a bit in the evening. Try not to skip a workout. But never run when you are anyway too tired. Also, the days you are stressed and don't feel like running, are the days you need it the most. So lace up and head out. You will come back happy.

2.   *Pacing:* The speed at which you run is very important. As distance runners, we run at an "easy" pace. This means that during long runs you should be able to make conversation fairly comfortably without feeling breathless. Once you find your pace, you will be able to sustain it over any distance. Speed work of course, is much faster.

3.   *Strength Training:* If you can include some amount of strength

and core workouts post your run, it will benefit your running tremendously. Plank, back strengthening, squats, lunges, crunches, hip and thigh exercises work well. This is not essential. Please do not let it overwhelm you. Do it only to take your running to the next level.

4.   *Post-run Stretching:* This is essential to prevent injuries resulting from tight muscles. It doesn't take time to do and can be done almost anywhere. Of course, we do look strange when we stretch on the side of a busy road. But then runners are crazy! Foam rolling is a great way to release the knots (like an expensive massage). So it may be worth investing in one once your running distance increases.

5.   *Running Buddy:* If you can run with a friend then that will ensure regularity. On days when you are lazy to get out of bed, and you know that your friend is waiting for you, you will have no choice but to hop out and move it. Also, as we run, we spend a lot of quality time together, which can build great friendships. Running with a group is a great way to find motivation as you see others running more or less than yourself.

6.   *MOST IMPORTANT:* Smile at all. Walkers. Runners. People who are sitting. We run because it makes us happy. Let us spread the joy.

When you come out of the storm, you won't be the same person who walked in.
That's what this storm's all about.

Kafka on the Shore – Haruki Murakami

MY RACES

Scmm 2005- *2:45*
Washington DC 10k- *67 mins*
Scmm 2006- *2:31*
Scmm 2007- *2:25*
Scmm 2008- *2:20*
Scmm 2010- *2:12*
Delhi 2010- *2:17*
Scmm 2011- *2:08*
Thane 2011- *02:03*
Pondicherry 2011- *2:21*
Dna womens 2011- *2:05*
Bangkok 10k- *56 mins*
Footsteps for good 10k: *63 mins*
Scmm 2012- full- *4:35*
Dna womens 2011- *2:05*
Borivali national park 2012- *2:04*
Scmm 2013- full- *4:33*
Hyderabad half 2013- *2:08*
Vasai- virar- half- *2013*
Scmm 2014- full- *4:09*
Satara 2014- *2:15*

CONTACT DETAILS

Every runner has a story. We would love to hear yours. Do share it with us- a write up and photographs if possible , and become a part of Team Running Soul.

Email: *parul@therunningsoul.com*
Website: *therunningsoul.com*

Please browse the website for our branded products like t shirts, motivational bookmarks, posters and more...